SUNTE~~

High-Wide
&
Mighty

A. E. Eaton.

© Copyright (A. E. Eaton.)

ISBN No. 0 9536331-1-X

First published in 2001
By ReCall Publications.

50,Turker Lane,
Northallerton.
North Yorkshire.
DL6 1QA
www.Recallpublications.co.uk
tony@eaton63.fsnet.co.uk

Printed by
Thurston Printers, 6 Amber Street, Saltburn-by-the-Sea, TS12 1DT
Telephone: 01287 623756
www.thurstonprinters.co.uk

Introduction

In the many books that I have read about Northallerton and the local districts, I have not come across any references to Sunter Brothers the heavy haulage company which for many years was based at Boroughbridge Road, Northallerton. Without doubt Sunter Brothers was the biggest private local employers in the area and gave work to many hundreds of men and women from the 1930s to its demise in 1986. Therefore I thought that a history of this outstanding company should be written as a tribute to Tom Sunter, Len Sunter, Joe Sunter and latterly Peter Sunter for their contribution to the local economy, their place in local history and the history of the heavy haulage industry nation wide. Local author Bob Tuck has written several excellent books on heavy haulage which in each edition he alludes to the Brothers' operations a great deal. Those well researched books give greater detail of the vehicles and the range of trailer specifications that were used by the heavy haulage companies than appears in this book. My story differs widely in that respect.

Sunters-High-Wide & Mighty, which starts its historical journey in 1890, is an anecdotal history and not the definitive history of the company. From the outset when researching this book, I decided that the story was to be told in a light and social style without too much emphasis on the internal machinations of big business, boardroom meetings or high technical specifications of vehicles and equipment. Within its pages I have included all members of the Sunter family, many of the disparate and interesting characters that have worked for the company and some of their many strange and amusing stories that they experienced over the years. Perhaps in the future, a definitive and more scholarly history might be written about Sunters, thus completing the whole story of a remarkable family and the drive and determination of the central figure in the entire saga-Tom Sunter.

Tony Eaton
Northallerton.
May 2001.

Cover Picture: The Rotinoff Atlantic passing down Linthorpe Road, Middlesbrough
Photo: Denis Wompra

ACKNOWLEDGEMENTS

My thanks go to the following for their help in the production of this book.

The Sunter family for their contributions;
Margaret Sunter, Audrey Sunter, Rosa Laurie (Sunter) for their memories of the early days, Peter Sunter for his personal recordings, Malcolm White for his detail of the family, George Percival for his family memories and Philip Muat for his decisive help and detail via the Sunter family genealogy.

Photographs reproduced by kind permission of;
Denis Wompra, Risbey Photography J.Boulton, Anthony Blake, J. Ayre, Hodgsons Photography Northallerton, British Steel, Head Wrightson, Foster & Wheeler, ICI/Zeneca, Sunters/ITM collection, Topcliffe Cranes, The Northern Echo, Malcolm Slater. The Cartoon reproduced by kind permission of the editor of the Truck & Driver Magazine. J. Ayre.

The scores of people who loaned personal photographs and documents without any time limit set for their return.
I would also like to thank that trio of senior employees, John Robinson, Philip Braithwaite (Snr) and Les Taylor for their memories of the early years, and all former employees of Sunter Brothers who volunteered their photographs, time and memories without whose help this book could never have been written.

A special thank you to Jack Bosomworth, Ken Wilson, Jacqueline and Malcolm White for their proof reading and their editing.

DEDICATION

I dedicate this book to all motorists who have had the misfortune to be held up by High-Wide & Mighty loads on the Queen's highway, to all the fascinated bystanders who witnessed the movement of such loads, and also to the men who manoeuvred those monstrous charges with such skill, dexterity and endurance.

CONTENTS

The Brothers Sunter

Tom - George - Len - Joe

The Swaledale Years

SUNTERS is a name that evokes memories of monstrous loads borne on multi wheeled trailers towed by equally gargantuan tractors under escort by a phalanx of motorcycle police outriders and a host of fascinated onlookers. It is a name that brings back yet more memories of sweating drivers and cursing steersmen coaxing and cajoling their unwieldy charges through the streets and around impossible corners of the towns and cities throughout the country. The name also awakens visions of angry and frustrated motorists venting their spleen on the trailer crews whilst hemmed in behind those slow moving leviathans. But for every frustrated motorist, an equal number of onlookers would be standing in awe at the sheer size of the loads being so skilfully manoeuvred. No more so were those memories more evident than on all roads leading to the High Street of the North Yorkshire market town of Northallerton, the home of this legendary company. Today alas, all that remains is the name and the memories of this one time giant of the heavy road haulage industry. No more do County Police Forces and Highways Authorities have to liaise and fret at having to route and control those monsters. No more do those mighty loads fill high streets and country roads alike. Although the company and the loads are no longer around, it is right that the name be remembered. However not only should the name of Sunter and all that it meant to the community be remembered, so should the names of the many scores of men and women who made it possible for those loads to be moved and delivered. Although they were renowned for their expertise in moving very high, very heavy and extremely awkward loads to apparently inaccessible and impossible locations, it was not always so. The Sunter story like many successful companies had a modest and unspectacular genesis, and for them that began before the turn of the twentieth century. The story of this outstanding company started in the hills and valleys of Swaledale in what was the old North Riding of Yorkshire where the name Sunter is known throughout many neighbourhoods. There were and are many families bearing this distinguished name in those parts of the county but yet, not all are related. The legend of this particular family began with the marriage of George Sunter to Alice Sunter in the year of 1890.

The Certificate that was to be the start of it all.

George Sunter, the patriarch of the family was born at Gunnerside near Richmond on the 6th of October 1864. His education began and ended at Gunnerside School with an education that was adequate, that is to say he could read, he could write and he was numerate. George never liked school and was known for his comments of exasperation each Friday when arriving home from School. He would throw his books down onto the table and say, "Monday will never come!" Yet, this education was deemed to be good enough for the life he was to lead as a Dalesman and farmer, albeit of modest means. Despite not liking school, George was very astute and numerate when dealing in any form of business. He was able to arrive at an answer from any given set of figures via two or three different routes, thus confirming the deal.

George met his future bride Alice Sunter the daughter of Thomas and Jane Sunter in the-mid 1880s when she was a girl still in her early teen-age years. Thomas Sunter was the local butcher in Gunnerside and both families were well known to one another. Alice was born in Gunnerside on the 12th of November 1872 and like her husband to be, attended the same school. After the usual courteous and decorous courtship, twenty six year old George and eighteen year old Alice were married by the Reverend Thomas Peers on the 27th of November 1890, in the Wesleyan Chapel at Reeth, their union doubly reinforcing the family name. With this doubling of the Sunter name, it seemed almost destiny that any offspring of that union would assuredly make their mark in the local community. George and Alice moved into the large and spacious but rented Mariton House in Gunnerside situated in the idyllic and undulating sheep dotted dry stone walled hills of Swaledale. The countryside although undeniably beautiful and serene, was a beauty and a serenity that hid the harshness and truth of the times and the long hours of wearying labour required to earn a basic living. From the turn of the century George earned his living as a 'Carrying Contractor' working for the Sir Francis Lead Mines of the upper Dales up Gunnerside Gill to the north of the village where lead ore was mined. It contained galena the lead-containing mineral, along with other minerals mainly barytes, fluorspar and chert. Lead ore had been mined since before Roman times but more actively after the seventeenth century.

One regular task for George whilst working for the mining company was for him to take a consignment of lead ore in his twin horse drawn cart and slowly plod toward the east coast. The distance of the journey was such that it required an overnight stop at Yarm where he discharged his load of ore and partook of a quantity of thirst quenching drinks. It was then on to his destination, the seaside town of Redcar. On reaching Redcar he would discharge his load of lead ore to the dealers, collect a quantity of gunpowder from a magazine built into the cliff sides, purchase a barrel of kippers and then retrace his journey with yet another overnight stop at Stockton. On returning to Gunnerside he would first see to his horses ensuring that they were watered and fed before thinking of his own needs. Then with all the resolution that typified the man and if there were time and need, he would walk some five miles or so up the moors to Wensleydale to do a deal for a calf and then walk back. In later years when he had sons of his own, he would give them the barrel

George and Alice Sunter.
Their marriage in 1890 was to be the start of the Sunter Story. They had ten children, six girls and four boys. Three of the boys, Thomas, Leonard and Joseph were all involved in the development and the expansion of the heavy haulage company - Sunter Brothers

of kippers with the order to go out and sell. They didn't dare come back until all the fish had been sold.

Within two years of their marriage Alice had given birth to the first of their children, nine more were to follow. The children were born at fairly close intervals, which kept Alice as a nursing mother well into her forty-first year. With the arrival of their first born, Dora, Alice was not only a farm-housewife, she was a mother, and with unstinting endeavour she set about her new tasks with a love and devotion that was her forte. Alice had many skills and from the time she became a mother there was one skill that she put to work almost immediately and that was the skill of sewing and making clothes. Almost all of the clothes the young Sunters wore were hand made. Many years later, Joseph Sunter was to recall how he would be woken in the middle of the night by his mother to be cajoled into trying on a particular garment that she had partially completed for him. All protests of sleepiness being waved aside as she fitted on the clothing. Being discomfited and pricked by pins was a hazard with which the Sunter children had to put up with whenever mother was sewing. Without fail every morning at 4.30 she would rise with her husband, go to the scullery and light the fires below two enormous metal bowls filled with water. This water was for the use of whole family and for the chores of washing and house cleaning for the rest of the day. Then it was breakfast with the children after which they both prepared for the rest of the day. There was one ritual that mother Sunter always adhered to in her routine of housekeeping and that was the changing of the carpets and curtains. Each Saturday, down came the weekday curtains and up would come the weekday carpet. The floor and fireplace would be scrubbed spotlessly clean, and then out would come the Sunday curtains and the carpet. By the Monday everything would be back to normal. In between these tasks while waiting for the scrubbed floor to dry, she would walk to her mother's house and do the housework for her and then return to complete her own.

The Sunter children like their parents attended the school in Gunnerside and like their parents worshipped at the Weslyan Chapel. Both Alice and George without pretension were practising Christians and raised their children in a home that had a strong Christian ethic. Life in the Dales although generally very hard work, was not all farming, housework and raising a family for George and Alice for they both had a great love of music and singing in particular. Alice had the gift of a beautiful singing voice and was a member of the Gunnerside Methodist Choir. She would often perform solos in and around the chapels of Gunnerside, and on occasion she would sing duets with her brother George. Although a housewife, Alice Sunter was a very literate person and won many book prizes when at school. These books were her pride and joy and were read from cover to cover. Her culinary skills were widely appreciated especially her famous cheese cakes which led to her being invited to do the catering for the Shortest Day Festival at Gunnerside. But yet, not only was her culinary famous, her dexterity with the needle and the art of quilt making was also equally well known in the Yorkshire Dales.

Although George Sunter was classed as a farmer, it was a very simple and basic type of farming that he followed. He utilised his land by growing grass and converting it into hay, which was then sold for fodder to the local sheep and cattle farmers. When hay time came around, neighbouring farmers and the whole family were employed to help gather in the hay, even the very young children of the family would help by treading down the hay to make it compact. Hard work to George Sunter was second nature; he was nothing if not a man of sterling character and unflagging industry. Although hard working and industrious and a loving family man, he was also a man of short temper and not for nothing was he known as 'Fire' Sunter, as anyone who felt the lash of his tongue would soon discover. However, he was given the sobriquet 'Fire' when as a child he accidentally set fire to his bed. With having a large family to feed, George and his wife would supplement their food by rearing a single pig, and then having it slaughtered for ham, pork and bacon after which George would then go to the market and purchase another for rearing. Seemingly the Sunter house was always adorned with freshly cured hams hanging by hooks from the ceiling.

With the closing down of the lead mines some years into the 1920s, another way to earn a living had to be devised by George and he set about the problem by expanding his business of buying and selling calves. He would travel to all parts of

**GUNNERSIDE,
RICHMOND, Yorks.**

192

M

B^{OUGHT}
.. OF **George Sunter,** Senior.

CALF DEALER.

A receipt from the calf dealing business.

Swaledale and Wensleydale buying calves at 7/- to 10/- per animal buying no more than two at any one time, he would then take them to the markets. The conveyance he used was a wonderfully named vehicle called a 'Shandrydan' which, according to George was a horse (Polly) drawn cart specially designed for the carrying of calves. The dictionary describes a shandrydan as a 'rickety old fashioned vehicle' Which ever it was and that was probably both, it suited the purpose and did the job.

Len Chapman of Stokesley a schoolboy in the 1920s remembers meeting George 'Fire' Sunter while the old man was on his rounds. He recalls his brother

Robert once telling him that he had been given a lift to school by George and during their conversation he was asked when did the school close for the holidays. Robert gave the first answer that came into his head 'tomorrow' he replied. The next day Robert came upon George Sunter in his 'shandra'. So vexed was George that he had been told a lie, he delivered a swift clip around Robert's ear for being untruthful That was the other side of 'Fire' Sunter.

In the Dales life at times could be fairly grim but there is one hilarious story involving George and Polly when they both were once returning to Gunnerside from one of their regular trips of calf collection and delivery. In Gunnerside there was a stone horse trough that was fed by a nearby stream and on arrival George would always give Polly her head and she quite naturally went to the trough. On one occasion as she bent her head to drink, a rat bit her on the nose causing her to rear up and gallop away helter skelter down into the village street galloping full tilt through the window of the 'Big Shop' with the rat still hanging on grimly to her nose. Luckily, neither Polly nor George were injured.

Although in general the people of the Dales were honest, God fearing and decent, from time to time their honesty could slip into a shade of venality. In the hill bottoms, lush grass grew in abundance but the grass on the hillsides was much hardier and was very difficult to mow. Irish hill workers were often hired for the job as they were hard working skilled 'scythesmen' who used a scythe that was theirs and theirs alone and the implement was guarded with a jealous pride. They would not allow anyone to so much as sharpen the blade. For this task they utilised ham fat and the sand from the bed of the nearby tarn to form a paste with which they then honed the steel blade to a razor sharp edge. Their pay was minimal but which also included a bed of hay in a barn, and food provided by the farmer's wife. There is a supposedly true story about a certain Dale's farmer who required a hillside of grass to be mowed and who hired an itinerant Irish worker to do the job. The particular Irishman hired by the farmer to cut the hardy grass on the hillside began his task of scything with a promise from the farmer that if he completed the job within a single day; he would receive a sovereign in addition to the normal pittance offered. By mid-day, he was more than well on the way to completing the work which was noticed by his employer. The farmer, realising that it was going to cost him a sovereign, told the worker that his wife would soon be bringing him a canister of tea. Meanwhile he had his wife mix a large dose of physic to the promised drink. The worker drank the tea with gusto and carried on working, and within no time the purgative began its work and troubled him immensely. The Irishman not to be done out of his reward, carried on working, taking periodic breaks to drop his trousers to answer the many calls of nature, then with Irish tenacity and resolution, got back to his work. He eventually received his sovereign at the end of the day, much to the chagrin of the farmer.

In the same vein, George Sunter was not above trying to make a few shillings on the shady side of honesty. On more than one occasion he had been known to negotiate for a calf in the local pub in Gunnerside and almost always it was done over a tot or two of rum, George's favourite tipple, hoping that the drink might beguile

Mariton House the first home of George and Alice Sunter.

Spring End the house occupied by Tom and Margaret Sunter.

the buyer and so fall for his next ruse. Both Tom and his father were quick calculators of figures and George was a renowned domino player for that reason. He played at the Punch Bowl in Low Row on Saturday evenings and invariably arrived home with his winnings, packets of Woodbines. He kept these in an old wooden bin in an outhouse with other little treasures. One day, the older sons tried to raid the locked bin by prising open the lid so that Len who had the thinnest arms could gain access. They heard their father's footsteps and made off but Len was trapped by his arm and had to face the consequences from his angry father. Another story worth repeating is about George trying to pull a fast one with a potential buyer, which entailed the proposed sale of a sheep dog. George would tell the customer that he could acquire for him a well trained dog, trained that is, in rounding up sheep. What he did not tell the buyer was that the dog had one serious shortcoming that it could not break. The dog that he produced was ideal at rounding up the sheep, but had the unfortunate trait of immediately scattering them to all corners. To counter this, George worked out a ruse that as soon as the dog had rounded up the sheep, he would immediately shout the command 'Divide!' The dog responded appearing to be obedient and well trained. This impressed the new owner and resulted in a sale.

As time passed, the Sunter children left that small school and began to find their way in the world. The early part of the twentieth century was for them fast changing times, not least the development of the motorcar and the world of transport in general. It was that industry that was to make the name Sunter famous nation wide.

The Sunter Children.

All the Sunter children were of strong character and showed many talents not least a musical one and each was to make his or her way through life in a variety of ways. Tom, the eldest of the boys was to show an unusual flare for business and an eye for an opportunity at a very early age. At this juncture of the story it must be stated that the main thrust of the narrative of the Sunter family story will be about the drive and business acumen of Tom Sunter, but with the caveat that; 'He was helped in many ways through life by his parents, brothers sisters his wife and friends, without whom he could never have succeeded in the way that he did'.

By the mid 1920s all but two of the Sunter children had reached maturity and in some cases were married with families of their own. The two exceptions were Joseph and Rosa who were still in their early teens.

Dora-the first child was born on the 26th of September 1892 and she married Norman McCombie who hailed from Glasgow. They had two children. Dorothy and Patricia.

Alice-the second eldest was born on the 4th of December 1894 and showed at an early age, the spirit and determination in which they were raised and what was to become the hallmark of the Sunter family. Mindful of the problems that young women faced in those days when trying to find employment within a small farming community such as Swaledale, Alice crossed the border into Lancashire. There she found work in, as she put 'In Service' at a 'Big House' in Colne where she worked for several years. Whenever her most welcomed week end of off duty came around, she would take the train from Colne to Askrigg and then walk over the 'tops' on to Swaledale and then into Gunnerside to be with her family, a good two hours of walking. After leaving Colne she worked for her two maiden aunts, Rose and Dora Sunter, (sisters to her mother) who jointly owned a bakery in South Bank (later Redcar. Not only was she to work in the bakery, she was also expected to do all the menial housework. One of her many chores was to scrub the step leading to the shop's entrance and this had to be done at 5.30 am. One morning she was carrying out this particular task when a certain John Muat passed by on his way to work. He gave the young Alice a nod; the nod was subsequently followed by a quiet 'Hello' then a chat and then an invitation for her to walk out with him. On the 30th of December 1918 they married at Gunnerside Church and set up home in Middlesbrough. They had three children. Elsie, Doreen and Philip. Doreen Muat was very talented musically and was to become famous locally for her soprano voice. (No doubt having inherited the talent from her grandmother) She qualified at the LRAM (London Royal Academy of Music) and sang in many musicals within the Cleveland area. She founded a Ladies Choir known as 'The Elizabethan Singers' a choir that is still going strong to this day. Philip went into engineering retiring as an Engineering Project Manager.

Mary was on born 18th November 1895 and like her sister Alice had a wonderful singing voice and won many competitions in the Burnley area. She met Edgar Hugill who hailed from Burnley and was the owner of a van and sold hardware in the town. Edgar showed his keenness when courting Mary, as he would cycle from Burnley to Gunnerside just to see his lady-love. They married and had a daughter Agnes.

Jane was born on the 7th October 1897 later to be known as Jenny, was the last child to be born before the turn of the century, met and married Wilfrid White on the 29th of September 1924. Wilfrid was the 2nd Engineer with the Merchant Marine, on the SS. Umona with Natal Line Steamers of Bullard King, and later qualified as Chief Engineer. He then left the sea and worked for Smith's Docks. On the 4th of January 1944 he was awarded the British Empire Medal (BEM) for his war work. Jane and Wilfrid had a son Malcolm, who eventually qualified as a Consultant Anaesthetist.

Thomas was born on the 8th of January 1900. He was to become the head of Sunter Brothers Haulage Company, but more of him later.

Leonard was born on the 25th July 1901 and was the second son and eventually he found work with Tunnicliffe Timber Merchants of Great Ayton near Stokesley. Len married Sybil Marsden a qualified nurse in 1933 and they had three children. Olga, Dorothy and Peter. Len and his son Peter will feature along with Tom as the story unfolds.

Isabel was born on the 7th February 1904, married Arthur Percival and they had one son, George Sunter. George was later to be involved with the haulage and coaching business but some years hence.

George was born on the 27th August 1906 and was the third of the Sunter sons, by the late 1920s had settled in Burnley having left Yorkshire with just 19/- in his pocket and went to live with his sister Mary and brother in law Edgar. He eventually found work in the motor trade and married Louisa. They had a son David who now lives in Virginia USA and like his father is in the motor trade.

Joseph Alderson was born on the 11th October 1909 and he met and married Audrey Thexton in 1943. They had a daughter Margaret. Joseph was the fourth of the brothers who was to be part of the trio of Sunter Brothers haulage business and was later to become the head of the coach business.

Rosamund was born on the 29th of January 1912 and was the only one of the children who did not go out and find work elsewhere. Rosa although still an early teenager by the 1920s, was devoted to her parents and decided that she was to be the one that would stay at home and help her mother run the household. Rosa eventually became nurse and home help when both of her parents became aged and infirm. Always known as Rosa, she was to marry much later in life.

Tom Sunter-Businessman.

Thomas Sunter the first son of the Sunter children was born on the 8th of January 1900. He was a man of moderate physical height, albeit well proportioned which embodied a muscular physique. These physical qualities genetic in origin were given impetus by the simple and balanced life living in the hill country and austere terrain of Upper Swaledale. Such conditions bred self discipline and improvisation. Schooled at Gunnerside and being born of farming stock he made it his duty to help his father with the many tasks on what in reality, was a small holding. One of the many jobs he undertook in the summertime was to fetch the cows down from the hillside to the byre for milking. He also helped by milking the cows and in the late summer collected bracken for the horse's bedding. For this task he would take a home built sledge to carry the mounds of bedding. Tom's father would often ask the local council road foreman for half a day's work breaking stones for road building. The stone used was limestone from the riverbed which had to be broken into egg sized pieces. The quantity was measured by the yard and built into pyramids for which he was paid 2/- the stones or aggregate was 'blinded' with mud covered by water from a water cart and then steam rolled. This was the method of road building in rural areas such as Swaledale until the mid 1930 when Tarmacadam became the norm.

It was 1913 when Tom left school and a little more than a year after his leaving, the First World War had begun its deadly business across Europe. With the advent of the war, the War Ministry ordered a vast expansion of military camps and installations throughout the country. Catterick Village situated but a few miles from Gunnerside was selected to take one such army camp. That is where Tom Sunter found his first job other than farm work. A Darlington based building company laying the roads to and from the camp and constructing buildings under contract to the War Ministry took him on. It was arduous work but one which gave him his first wage packet and the real value of having a job.

Later, he was employed by the War Ministry working for the ACC (Army Canteen Corps) the forerunner of the NAAFI, and it was with the ACC that he learnt to drive. As the war went into its fourth year, the manpower shortage for the army was at an extremely critical stage and to compensate the age limit for conscription was lowered to eighteen years. Tom who was born in the last year of the nineteenth century became eligible for call-up and in the summer of 1918 he was duly drafted into the ASC (Army Service Corps.) The ASC was the transport corps of the British Army and anything that had to be moved was moved by the ASC and that is when Tom's ability to drive was utilised. Fortunately he was not sent to France as by the time he had completed his basic army training it was almost November and the war was rapidly coming to its very welcome conclusion. After completing his army training, he was posted to Ireland for a few months where he not only drove lorries but also rode a motorcycle combination. It was while he was in Ireland that he saw his first aeroplane and he was so taken by the sight of the flying machine that he drove his motorcycle into a crowd of people who themselves were watching the aeroplane. Fortunately there were no injuries. From Ireland he was sent to Portsmouth where he completed his military service in mid 1919. On leaving the army, Tom Sunter was employed as a driver for a transport firm in Lancashire, but after two years in the job he left and returned to his native Gunnerside. He then found a job as a bus driver or more appropriately a 'Charabanc' driver with George Metcalfe of Reeth, running the Richmond-Keld service, the job again lasting for two years.

It was after this job that Tom Sunter began to suffer all the signs and symptoms of diabetes mellitus, a debilitating disease that was nearly to cost him his life. It was well known that Tom had what was described as a sweet tooth and a thirst for sweet drinks and he indulged in these passions to a far greater degree than he really ought. He would regularly visit a sweet shop in nearby Richmond to buy sweets from the shopkeeper who was more than willing to sell them to him. His family doctor,

Tom as a civilian driver with ACC at Catterick Camp in 1917

Len in repose c 1920

George 'Fire' Sunter with George and Tom.

Haytime, When all the family joined in.
Tom - George - Isabel - Jenny - Rosa - Mary - George Senior

Five of the Sunter girls.
Jenny - Mary - Alice - Isabel - Dora

Four Sons in Law with George Sunter
(centre) Edgar Hugill - Norman Mc Combie
Arthur Percival - Wilfrid White

Len Sunter - Willy Shaw (Publican) - Tom Sunter - Tommy Brown (Postman)

William Speirs, immediately recognised the onset of the diabetes and set about trying to control it dietetically, but Tom was less than co-operative and still tended to eat sweet foods. This had a disastrous effect on his health, which eventually caused him to become very weak and debilitated. The only course left was to try a new medical breakthrough in the treatment of diabetes. In 1921 two Canadians named Banting and Best discovered the hormone named insulin, which was found to be a remedy for the problems of diabetes mellitus, but did not cure it. Insulin given via injection before food helps to control the sugar within the body's system. This discovery was a milestone in medical treatment and was to save countless lives. Dr. Speirs suggested that Tom should be immediately given this new treatment. That was when Tom's will power and beliefs came to the fore. He simply refused to take the treatment thinking that insulin was a drug, when in fact it is a hormone, as any form of drugs was generally considered wrong and he would have no part of it. He could not and would not be convinced otherwise. He carried on with the diet control but clearly it wasn't working and his health declined dramatically. Tom had a cousin by the name of Tom Huss who also lived in Gunnerside who was acquainted with a qualified nurse who had been trained at St. Mary's Hospital London, the Fever Hospital Nottingham and the Infirmary in Newcastle. Her name was Lucy May Allan known colloquially as 'Dimp' because of the dimples on her cheeks. Dimp was to play a leading part in the saving of Tom's life.

Tom's parents approached her explaining that Tom was becoming weaker by the day and spent more time in bed than out and asked if she could help. Dimp agreed and went to see Dr. Speirs and asked if Tom could be given insulin a new substance she had heard about when she was at Newcastle. Dr. Speirs agreed but warned Dimp that Tom had refused it previously believing it to be a drug. Eventually Tom became comatose and so Dimp asked the doctor if she could administer the insulin. He agreed but said it didn't matter what he was given as he was almost past help. That same evening while Dimp was giving Tom his first injection of insulin, Alice his mother knelt in prayer by his bedside. She remained praying for him almost continuously. At 5.30 in the morning Tom slowly opened his eyes and uttered one word 'Mother!' He then asked her the time and when he was told, he replied 'Well I'll go to Kent!' this being a local phrase to show surprise. He then began to regain his conscious state. Dr. Speirs who lived in Reeth enquired of a villager how Tom was doing and was astounded to learn that he had regained consciousness. The tenacity and beliefs of Dimp had paid off; Tom was on the mend. Rehabilitation was Tom's next hurdle because of weakness and wasting of his limbs particularly his legs. He was unable to walk but with continued insulin therapy he began to regain some limb movement. With the assistance of two of his sisters Isobel and Rosa and his niece Dorothy, he began to use his legs tottering along the High Green at the front of Mariton House supported by the girls. A local Masseur by the name of Mr. Ward was called into help and he managed to improve muscle tone in Tom's legs until he could walk normally. Once his strength had returned he was taught to inject himself with the insulin before meals which he did into his left arm-unseen.
Once Tom had fully recovered from the trauma of the coma and the shock of the onset of diabetes, he set about earning a living but this time he was to be the one in

charge. It was now 1928 and it was at this time of his life that Tom's in-built talent for spotting a business opportunity came to the fore. In those early days, the movement of cattle and sheep to markets was by the simple method of driving the animals over the moor to the market, those not sold, were driven back. Tom was conscious of seeing those sheep and cattle arriving back in a state of exhaustion and decided that there must be a better way of doing it. He persuaded his father to loan him a sum of

'Dimp'
Nurse Lucy May Allan
who saved Tom's life
by the use of insulin

Tom

Tom with his mother.

money with which to buy a motor vehicle to transport the animals into Wensleydale and back. The vehicle he bought was a left-hand drive American Model T Ford. Realising that he lived in a very beautiful part of the county and that there were people of comfortable means who wished to visit his part of the Yorkshire Dales and this led to an idea. Although there was a reasonably good train service to the Dales, other forms of public transport were sparse and sporadic. Not only was the public transport sparse it was also very uncomfortable. The Ford T was a relatively spacious car and could seat six persons with ease and comfort. With this and a modicum of hope, Tom Sunter set out on his first commercial enterprise. As the chauffeur, he would take parties of tourist to the beauty spots and the tiny hamlets where they would admire the view and stop for refreshments at the village tea-rooms in and around the Dales. So began Tom's first business venture in transport.

Not only did he carry tourists with the Model T Ford; he also took on his first commercial haulage contract at this time. He was approached to deliver a sideboard from Gunnerside Village to Newcastle on Tyne for a negotiated fee of £5 for the entire journey. To accommodate the sideboard the bodywork was 'adjusted' to be able to take freight and also live stock. The back of the Ford was removed to form what might be described as a Pick-Up truck. They set off with the sideboard and a goodly supply of spare tyres as tyres in the early days of motoring were notoriously unreliable and were very prone to puncturing. They delivered the sideboard but not without a flurry of punctures on the way there and back. They ran out of 'good tyres' and had to resort to stuffing grass in the punctured ones to give them some sort of soft running and road holding until they arrived back at Gunnerside. A precarious first 'long distance' run, but an important one. So the Model T Ford was not only for carrying tourists, but also for carrying freight and livestock, and this was the precursor to Sunter's Haulage Business. Tom, with the help of Len and Joss ran this enterprise for almost five years, building up capital, and it must be said commercial know how and not a little confidence.

The felling of timber was big business in the local area and the means of transporting the long poles was by horse drawn wagons. Tom applied for a contract with Hird and Gibson Timber Brokers and a deal was struck. For the three brothers this was the real opportunity that they needed to begin a proper heavy haulage business. Hauling the timber by a team of horses was slow and difficult work and placed great strain on the shire horses used for the hauling. Although the motor wagon had been in use in the urban areas for many years, horses were still the mainstay of transport in the farming communities of the country in the mid 1920s. Although work was plentiful, Tom realised that in the timber hauling business, the means with which to get the felled timber to its point of delivery was the big drawback to an efficient haulage business. He had to make a decision to change from real horsepower to mechanical horsepower. This he set about with his usual determination.

Sunter Brothers Ltd.

In 1931 Tom and his brothers got rid of the T Ford and sold the horse drawn transport to Derek Guy of Keld and then bought two lorries, a Bedford and an American Chevrolet. With the use of motor driven transport, the speed of timber felling and despatch increased dramatically. It was then that they realised an assistant was needed to help with the workload and they took on a fifteen year old youth by the name of John Robinson who hailed from Northumberland but lived with his parents in the Punch Bowl Inn at Low Row, a village close to Gunnerside. Little did they realise that that mild mannered youth was to stay with them for more than fifty years and develop into a first rate heavy tractor driver and a first class employee. John's first job with the Sunter Brothers was leading coal to the isolated farmsteads in Swaledale and Wensleydale. He does not remember exactly how much he was paid when he first began working for them, but he seems to think it was something in the order of 2d per hour, which equated to approximately 100 pence in old money. With 12 pence to a shilling, John was paid 8/4d which is approximates to 41 1/2 new pence.

Some time later there were three vehicles on the strength of the company, all Chevrolets each having an interchangeable body. This allowed the vehicles to either carry furniture in a van style body, or general goods on a flat body. Although timber hauling (pit props to the Yorkshire coalfields) became their main source of work, through seasonal or unseasonable events work dropped off. The ever-resourceful Sunter brothers carried on delivering every kind of goods. Anything that needed to be transported in the local area was taken on, whether it be, coal, calves, timber, furniture, nothing was ever turned down, but the transporting of timber was the chief source of work. For the transporting of cattle, trailers had to be built according to what ever was being transported, e.g. calves, or full-grown beasts. Building those trailers was time consuming and extremely hard work. The basic trailer was a standard flat model (for leading hay and straw) with lift up sides. When cattle were to be transported, the sides were lifted up and a top placed on with a ramp for the beasts to climb. If it were sheep, then a second deck had to be built with the floor overhanging the cab of the lorry. The sheep then would have to be coaxed and cajoled into the truck especially to the higher deck. John recalls that with the upper deck overhanging the cab, from time to time a shower of bovine urine would often cascade on to him and his windscreen.

Although the brothers were busy building up the business, it didn't stop them meeting girls and having fun. Len met Sybil Marsden a qualified nurse and even went one step further than having fun; by marrying her in 1933 and setting up home in Northallerton.

By 1935 there was an increase in timber leading for the brothers so the cattle transporting side of the business was eventually sold off, Tom realising that such diversity was not in the best interests of the company. It was also in that year that

Sunter Brothers gained the protection of being a Limited Company. After relinquishing the cattle delivery business, they acquired a contract for the collection and delivery of road gravel chippings. One contract the brothers had acquired was with the local Highway's Authority in Richmond delivering gravel and solid bitumen blocks to the various sites. John Robinson recalls driving to Richmond railway station where he was required to shovel a load of gravel from a high sided railway truck into his own truck. The longer he shovelled, the lower he sank into the rail truck, making the whole task that much more difficult. Once the load had been moved from the rail truck into the lorry, he would then have to go and dispense heaps of gravel at regular intervals along a particular stretch of highway. Gravel leading was the job he hated most.

George Sunter Junior with a horse drawn delivery accompanied by Mildred Pybus.
Mildred was a constant companion of the older Sunter Brothers. c 1930

Tarmacadam being laid at gunnerside
outside Mariton House. c 1935
The newly installed Shell Mex petrol pump
for
The Sunter business can be seen.

george-len tom

Tom sitting behind the wheel of the Model T Ford, his first mode of transport.
Sitting next to Tom is Mildred Pybus and a friend.
Len and George are in the back with a third girl. c 1928

Tom standing next to
Nelly Henderson
with one of his 'Dales Tours Car'.

Tom on a Dales Tour.

The Leyland pole wagon
used for timber hauling

William Percival next to his Standard 9 outside the shop window that
George Sunter and Polly broke after their headlong dash through Gunnerside

John Robinson
and Len Sunter
with a load of timber.
Len is wearing a cast off
United Bus Co. overcoat.

Len and Sybil Sunter on their wedding day 1933

By the early thirties Tom had recovered from his brush with death and saw the opportunity for felling and leading timber from Arkengarthdale, a small dale immediately to the north of Swaledale. A school friend, Tom Milner, was engaged in the wood yard at Reeth where timber led by Sunters from the Stang Forest was cut into pit props for the mines. This friend offered Tom the facilities for constructing a pole wagon in order to carry forty-foot lengths of timber. This consisted of hitching a long pole to what was known as the Sunter fifth wheel coupling. The fifth wheel was a heavily greased steel plate with a large railway sleeper centre pinned onto the plate. A pole (tree trunk) was attached to the fifth wheel sleeper by 'L' shaped brackets. The opposite end of the pole was a cannibalised Dennis back axle. The terrain where

John worked was the worst possible for tyres, but the ever resourceful Sunters got over that problem by 'relieving the local bus company of their worn out tyres. Within the next two years, not only had the amount of work and number of contracts increased, so had the range and distances travelled by the lorries for delivery and the number of staff on the pay roll. New arrivals were Jack Stout, Jimmy Fletcher, Jack Thompson, Joe Alderson, and Dick Helm. All were drivers or labourers. The company's chief mechanic was Bob Stubbs who later was to work for Kellet and Pick Motor Dealers of Northallerton. Not only was there an increase in staff, the number of vehicles had also increased and by the late 1930s the fleet consisted of, 2xBedfords, a Leyland (articulated pole trailer) and an Albion. A vintage Dennis was cannibalised and the spare axle parts were utilised to build a trailer chassis. Delivering timber to Rotherham in the south Yorkshire coalfields was how John Robinson learned his craft of driving long distance. It wasn't just driving; it was the skill of manoeuvring the long and unwieldy Leyland wagon in and out of the forest with a ninety-foot timber pole to control. This skill was to stand John in good stead for the future.

The timber hauling became very successful and Tom found time to indulge in a long held passion, that of sport and speed. In 1934 he purchased the first of a succession of high performance sports cars, a black SS1 (Standard Swallow) coupe the first in a long line of high speed sport and racing cars to be intermingled with elegant Rolls Royces and graceful Bentleys. At that time SS was not owned by Jaguar but by a smaller private company. Despite this it was a stylish low-slung car and sported a one and a half litre engine with a renix hood and red interior. Indeed this rare sight of a sports car in Swaledale drew the attention of a farmer's wife when it was standing outside a cow house and prompted her to say to Tom 'Aye Thomas, wat a lang neb its gitten' A year later he sold the SS1 and bought an SS100 which did have the famous Jaguar trade mark of leaping cat. This car was by far much faster than the SS1 and Tom's love of speed increased with the driving of his new acquisition. In 1939 Tom acquired a three and a half litre Drop Head, AVN 451, with a six-cylinder engine, a car that was not quite so outlandish and special. He enjoyed the handling of this car because he said it was so well balanced and simply felt right perhaps an unscientific comment but Tom's assessment depended so much on the look and feel of a vehicle.

Rented along with Mariton House some 100 yards distant was the Garth immediately adjacent to stone built stables, a piggery and housing for farm equipment. There was standing room for two vehicles, which required cover. Arthur Percival, Tom's brother-in-law was a stonemason by trade and a particularly skilled and versatile worker. He, his wife Isobel and their son George lived in Askrigg over in Wensleydale. Tom asked Arthur if he could extend the stone buildings and roof the area for a vehicle repair shed. This he did using corrugated sheeting and later excavated a pit to facilitate chassis and mechanical repairs. Joseph a willing worker was able to keep the mechanics and chassis of the vehicles in good repair and whilst Tom was an innovator, he did not practice mechanics as Joseph did. Leonard probably occupied a mid position and was not well practised in mechanics but more in haulage. Of the three brothers each had their individual skills, which integrated well. The Garth bungalow now stands where the repair workshop stood and is the home of Rosa.

Tom Sunter was a strong chapel man and sometimes his beliefs and principles showed in his work. One rule that he insisted upon (in the early days) was that no work should ever be carried out on a Sunday. One driver, Jack Stout was to find out about this strict ruling when he tried to work a Sunday run. Jack and John Robinson had prepared a load ready to go to the Middlesbrough area by a Saturday evening but not to leave until early Monday. Jack, who hailed from that area, decided that he would go first thing on the Sunday morning to get a head start and to get home. He duly carried out his intentions. When Tom heard of it he immediately gave Jack his marching orders. Once again as was the wont of the Sunter Brothers, Tom relented and reinstated Jack, but with a stern warning.

Being an expanding company, Tom realised that it was no longer a viable or sensible thing to operate out of Gunnerside so he decided to look for business premises that would be more central to the needs of the business. Although loads were being delivered to most parts of the United Kingdom, the bulk of the work was still in the northeast and Scotland. Because of that he looked for a site that would give him quick access to the major trunk road in the region, namely the A1 or The Great North Road as it was called in those early days. After searching the local area, a site in Northallerton was selected. On the outskirts of the town a site close to the railway crossing on what is known as Boroughbridge Road became available which suited the purpose. Tom made enquires to the law firm who were the selling agents and was asked to make an offer for the site. Although Sunter Brothers was a successful firm, they did not have ready capital to purchase land. Not to be outdone, Tom made what he considered to be an utterly ridiculous offer and to his astonishment it was accepted The site purchase was actually part of a larger site and a portion was already occupied by Sam Turners, the well known local farm supplies company. There was however ample room for a burgeoning road haulage company with a large fleet. By mid 1937 the move from sleepy Gunnerside to Northallerton had been completed.

In 1938 the business had expanded to such a degree that another worker had to be taken on for the timber hauling. A young fourteen-year-old boy by the name of Philip Braithwaite applied for the job and, like John Robinson before him, it was to be the start of a long association with the company. At the time Philip joined the company, a timber contract at Arkengarthdale near where Philip lived had been secured and he began his working life as a chain and cable boy, eventually graduating to tractor driving. The tractors used in the timber felling business were of the caterpillar-tracked variety as the agricultural types were of no use in dense wooded areas where traction was everything. To facilitate the transporting of the timber a new vehicle was purchased; a Scammel articulated pole wagon. This was a vast improvement on the Bedford and International. As the supply of timber was exhausted in one area, so then a fresh supply was found and that was at Coxwold a village at the foot of the Hambleton Hills, the timber being felled from the woods at the nearby Hall.

Although Tom Sunter was by nature a man with built in business acumen and a shrewd sense of what might be a good deal and what might not, he also had an eye for modernity. Swaledale like many other parts of Yorkshire and indeed many parts of the country was not yet linked to the national grid to receive electricity. While others in the Dale seemed to be content with their lot of Tilley Lamps, candles and other forms of lighting, Tom was determined that his household was to have electric power in one form or another. He paid a visit to Dove's Electricals of Darlington for advice on the installation of domestic electricity. The result was the purchasing of a diesel engine connected to 25 batteries producing 50 volts, the whole set up being installed into an out building at Mariton House. The series of batteries provided enough electricity to light the entire house and run a small refrigerator. This without doubt made life much more comfortable for all at Mariton. A short time after the installation of electric power, several people in the village expressed an interest in having the same for their houses. Within the next few months, nine more homes were connected up to the diesel engine at Mariton House and very soon overhead cables festooned the street of Gunnerside. (No such refinements as underground cables in those days) Dorothy McCombie who lived with Granda and Grandma Sunter at the house and who was the daughter of Norman and Dora (Sunter) McCombie was given the job of collecting the rent for the electricity. Dorothy recalls she had great difficulty in extracting the money from the customers, as the wont of some people is to delay payment for as long as possible. They told the young rent collector that they would only pay a responsible adult member from Mariton House. The installation of electric power to the house was an indication of the forward thinking of Tom Sunter, and this ability was to show time and again in the coming years.

Expansion was the key word for Sunter Brothers and by 1938 they were delivering steel from Tees-side to various parts of the northeast. The Leyland pole wagon although up to the task, it was obvious that the company needed fresh tractor motive power. In that same year, the first ever new vehicle purchased by Tom was added to the Sunter stable. This was an ERF (EPY 432) powered by a Gardner engine and nicknamed the 'Big Bomber'. Although running as a rigid, it also ran as a pole articulated wagon, which gave it great stability. As welcome as the new vehicle was, it proved to be a handful when the engine had to be started as it did not have an electric starter motor which apparently was an optional extra in those early days. John became very expert at starting the ERF's diesel engine by the use of a length of rope but only with the help of his wife Mary holding on to the other end.

The increase in steel delivery orders was to increase even further as the 1930s came to an end. In 1939 war with Germany once more cast its gloom over the country and with it all that it meant in the redistribution of manpower into the armed forces and industry. Road haulage was to play a big part in the war effort and as such, Sunter Brothers were to be part of that effort. Len and Joss Sunter were considered too old for military call up and of course Tom had served in the Great War but was not physically fit due to his diabetes. Driver John Robinson although eligible was considered to be in a reserved occupation and so stayed with the company. With the vast expansion of the war industry, orders for delivery by road were readily available. At this stage genuine heavy haulage was the domain of Wynns of South Wales and Sunters had only the capacity and capability to deliver relatively light loads. The work in the timber industry continued but was vastly expanded due to defence building. The steel industry was also placed on maximum output for the building of ships, tanks and a myriad of military hardware. Many of the loads carried by Sunters were aeroplane fuselage parts and steel sections for ship's hulls and keels. With the onset of war delivery, the work for the drivers became a daily grind of load up, deliver and get back to the depot. Not only was the actual work heavy going, but also the conditions in which they had to carry it out were somewhat restrictive. The 'blackout' rules were vigorously enforced by over zealous policemen and ARP wardens. Travelling by night in the winter months was almost an impossibility with the restrictions on the illumination a vehicle was allowed to project. The pay for a 48 hour week in the mid 1940s at Sunters was £4.12s. Tom Sunter offered a piece rate of an extra £3 for difficult loads being moved from the northeast to Scotland. It was reasonable money, but it was hard graft. There weren't too many complaints from the drivers as there were hundreds of thousands of men who were putting their lives in danger fighting the war, and their pay was minimal.

During the war there was a need for certain minerals to help with the war industries. One of those was barytes once found in the lead mining of Swaledale at the turn of the century. Tom considered that it might be worthwhile re-opening the lead mines at Old Gang situated between Swaledale and Arkengarthdale. After taking expert advice from a geologist and mineralogist in Newcastle he was tempted to go ahead with the business venture. Joseph became engaged in the work also but after a year, production was scant and the venture was considered not worthwhile and the mine closed down.

Back in Gunnerside, life at Mariton House went on as usual, but with the added company of two grandsons, George Percival, son of Isabel who also carried the name Sunter as his second Christian name and Philip Muat son of Alice, both boys were to spend many holidays with their grandparents in their early years. As almost all grandchildren do, they recall happy days playing on the farm and always remember the smell of home cooking and delicious meals.

At this time George senior continued to run his calf - carrying business of his own using a horse and cart as the means of transport but he was always on the lookout for more work. Tom's ingenuity began with the converting of a car into a pick-up and it continued with a simple idea. He converted a horse drawn mowing machine into a mechanical one by the simple expedient of removing the back wheels of a car and having the power drive taken up to the mower. Although this was Tom's idea, it is only fair to say that it was Jim Robinson who ran a garage in Grinton who carried out the actual mechanics and building of the thing. With this 'invention'

Tom Sunter secured a contract for grass cutting at an estate in at Satron. Later there was a need to move his 'invention' to a new location, but it had to be towed, as it did not have insurance or road tax. He attached the contraption to his car by a length of rope and got his eight year old nephew George Percival to steer it as he towed it along the country roads. The journey took them through Grinton and Low Row. At Low Row, Tom spotted a policeman just in time to stop and let the 'danger' pass. That was quite an introduction to driving for the young George.

For Tom there was another even closer encounter with a policeman, but this was in Gunnerside village. At his garage Tom kept a store of eggs and butter that he used to sell. He noticed that the supply of eggs etc was going down very rapidly and couldn't fathom out why. He asked his mother, but she hadn't taken any nor had his father. He decided to keep vigil in the out building where they were stored. With a pillow and couple of blankets he sat in his car and waited. In the early hours the door creaked open and in crept the village policeman in uniform who then began to help himself to a clutch of eggs. Tom confronted him and the shocked policeman burst into tears and pleaded not to be reported. Tom reprimanded him but forgave him with a warning. Tom decided not say anything as the policeman had a couple of children and he knew he would be ruined. The policeman thanked him and that was the end of it. Some time later the policeman was moved to Barnard Castle and he was caught doing a similar thing and was arrested, charged and given a prison sentence. A sad ending, which Tom had tried to avoid.

Due to the expansion in war work for the Sunter Brothers, another worker was taken on. Les Taylor was a seventeen-year-old youth in 1942 and was given a job by Tom Sunter when he was attending the young lads' father's funeral. Les Taylor's mother and Tom's father were brother and sister and so Les was the nephew of Tom. After the service Tom was talking to Les and his mother and remarked, "I could use a young lad like him" and offered Les a job there and then. Until then Les had been working as an assistant gamekeeper near Leeds and delivering milk not in bottles but via the use of a measuring ladle. The mode of transport was a pony and a two-wheeled cart. He accepted the job and was sent to work at Ripon where Sunters had a contract with John Spence Timber Merchant. Les's wage was £2.10/- per week with another fifty bob for his lodgings, which were located in a nearby pub. He was working alongside another seventeen year old, Philip Braithwaite, who by then was an 'old hand' having previously started work in 1938. The working conditions proved to be extremely hard and the hours long. His first job in the timber was as a 'chain/cable lad' which meant him having to haul the chain and the cable to the fallen timber for removal by winch and tractor. There was no such thing as extra padding for shoulders or gloves for that matter. His introduction to the timber business for Les was quite traumatic. A root of a tree was being forced out of the ground by the tractor when a large piece of root suddenly shot from the ground and struck Les on the head. He was groggy for a couple of hours and had a very sore head.

The work was extremely hard and at the end of a shift which was some ten hours long, his shoulders, arms and hands would be red raw and scratched with the handling of the steel cables. He was usually given most week ends off from Saturday afternoons to Sunday night and his train fare home was provided by his employer, but after a few weeks the money for the train fare didn't materialise, so the young Les had to face a boring time on his own. Les has his own thoughts of in whose pocket his train fare ended up, but he is reluctant even to this day to say. In the summer he used to join the rest of the men doing a few hours of hoeing for a local farmer, but the money he earned was almost immediately spent in the local pub. Eventually Les was taught how to drive a tractor and so his work became a little less arduous and bit more interesting. His job was to haul the timber out of the wood and take it to the winch where it was loaded onto one of the pole wagons to be hauled away.

A Timber Measurer who took regular measurements along the trunk's length assessed the timber being cut for cubic footage and weight. In that same year, Sybil Sunter gave birth to her third child a boy whom they christened Peter. Peter Sunter was destined to play a big part in the future development of the company.

Although Tom Sunter was busy building up his business, he still had time for many activities in and around Gunnerside. One such activity was acting as what one might describe as a 'Disc Jockey' long before that term was ever heard of. In the village hall at Gunnerside he organised dances for the local girls and the soldiers from Catterick Camp. Tom provided a good supply of dance music with the use of a wind-up gramophone. Those dances were a resounding success and were to lead to many romances and marriages. So popular and successful were those dances that Tom was to meet the girl at such a dance who was to later to become his wife. Margaret Parker was a twenty-five year old girl from Long Eaton in Derbyshire who was paying a summer visit to relatives in Gunnerside area. She went to one of the

A sketch of a Sunter International being loaded with timber at Ripon. c 1943

Joseph and Audrey Sunter on their wedding day 1943

Tom and Margaret on their wedding day 1944
The Best Man is George Sunter, the bridesmaids are; Rosa, Dorothy (cousin), Ruth (friend)

Mallie

Ann

The Christening of Ann.
Alice and George Sunter, Arnold Parker, Ann, Tom and Margaret Sunter, Florence Parker

Rosa on her wedding day with her brother Tom who gave her away.

Alice (Sunter) Muat

dances run by Tom where they were introduced to one another and that was the start of their romance. In the meantime, Joss had met and married Audrey Thexton a girl from Epsom and they married in 1943. They had one daughter whom they called Margaret. Tom and Margaret Parker married in 1944 and had two daughters, Ann and Mallie. As Margaret was a trained secretary, Tom set her to work at the office in the depot at Northallerton, but she doesn't recall doing very much or ever being paid for her work. Not only did Margaret and Tom meet at one of those dances, Rosa the youngest of the family, met her future husband Alexander Laurie who was in the army stationed at Catterick. It was at this time Tom acquired yet another sports car, this time it was a British Racing Green 14 HP open topped two seater Aston Martin. It can be said that Sunters edged into the heavier moving side of the industry when they bought their first low loader trailer in 1943 with which they carried relatively heavy loads. This however was only a very basic move into the heavy haulage business and the norm was with the usual lighter articulated loads. With orders for war materials ever increasing, Sunters was employed delivering an ever expanding demand for steel, timber, ships' parts, aircraft wings and fuselages all in support of the war effort. With this increase in the size of the loads and the distances travelled, the learning of routes was very rapidly ingrained into the drivers. By 1944 Les Taylor and Phil Braithwaite had been taught to drive and both went on to the timber delivery side of the business. Like Philip, Les Taylor was exempt military service as many heavy haulage drivers were classed as essential war workers.

As the business settled into its new depot at Boroughbridge Road, Tom Sunter invested in another diversification, although it was one in which he did not publicise a great deal. At the transport yard, he built a pigsty in which he installed several young pigs. It was wartime and rationing was the order of the day, with food and clothing coupons required for almost every basic need in life. A minuscule amount of meat per person per week was the basic allowance, which was not nearly enough. That is where Tom and many like him provided that little extra. Tom had the pigs fed and then had one slaughtered in the yard, have it butchered and then sold it to who ever would buy. All of this was quite illegal, as there were strict controls over the number of animals that could be slaughtered, so in short, Tom was dabbling in the 'Black Market'. A lot has been said about the Black Market and about the sort of people who engaged in that illicit business. But it is fair to say that the Black Marketeers did provide a service for those luxuries that were being denied due to the war. It was against the law, but one would hardly call them criminals. Most certainly high profits were made, but due to the risks being taken, few people complained about the price that they were asked to pay. Tom carried on this questionable activity till the end of rationing after the war. There are a couple of hilarious tales of Tom, and his 'special' meat sales. On one occasion he was to meet a contact at a certain garage where they were to exchange meat and money. When Tom arrived at the rendezvous point, there was a police car waiting. Tom hung around, for the police to go, but it stayed. After considerable agitation and thought, Tom approached the police and asked them why they were hanging around. It transpired that they were waiting for someone to bring them some 'special' meat. Another time a couple of policemen came to the yard and entered the office and asked to see Tom Sunter asking if it were true that he was selling ham and pork on the Black Market. When Tom admitted as much, the policemen told him that they would like to purchase a quantity. Although the police were under obligation to pursue such activities and often did, there was an under-current of feeling that although that sort of thing was illicit, it was not truly criminal.

Although there is a lot of humour in the haulage business, there was always a darker side. By and large and considering the type of loads and the conditions of the roads during the war to say nothing of lighting restrictions, accidents did happen from time to time. John Robinson was passing through Otterington with a Bedford pole wagon and a consignment of timber when he was involved in what turned out to be a fatal accident. As he passed the cross roads of Otterington Village a few miles out of Northallerton, a young man, (who will remain nameless) riding a motorcycle combination, drove straight out of the Thornton Le Moor junction and crashed into the rear wheels of John's Bedford. The force of the impact bent the metal timber stays of the pole wagon and naturally the young man was killed instantly. John was exonerated of any blame, but it was a sad episode for both the boy's parents and for John.

Post War - The Heavy League

In 1945 the whole of the nation welcomed the ending of the war and looked forward to peace and the long hard process of the rebuilding and redirection of industry from a war footing to peacetime diversity. War work was to be eventually wound down which meant that companies who had relied on orders from the various War Ministries, would have to jostle and compete for work and orders with every other company engaged in that field of business, not least the road haulage industry. Without doubt, the most significant dates in 1945 were May and August that signalled the end of the war with Germany and Japan. However, there was another date, which was to have a very great impact on almost every large industry in the country, and that date was when the result of the general election held in the summer of 1945 was announced. On the 26th of July in a landslide victory, Labour was elected as the government of the UK. As nationalisation was the linchpin of their strategy, the take over of almost all major industries by the government was inevitable. The railways, steel and the utilities such as electricity and gas were all to go under. The nationalisation of these industries is well documented and generally well known. However, the nationalisation of the road haulage industry, which is equally well documented, very little is public knowledge. With the take over into what was euphemistically called the 'Public Sector' Sunter Brothers and many companies like them were to feel the full weight of government interference and control. Although the future in many ways looked bright, ahead lay many perplexing problems to be faced before the business could expand in the direction the brothers were planning.

Back in Gunnerside, things went on in the normal steady way for George and Alice Sunter who were by now retired and taking things easy. Nine of the Sunter children had left home and made their own way into the world. The tenth child Rosa had remained to look after her ageing parents, especially her father who by then was suffering from gangrene in his legs and was becoming immobile. Realising the effort she was putting into the task of caring for their parents, Tom made her a director of the company and gave her an allowance to compensate for her not being able to go to work of her own volition. By 1947 'Granda' Sunter's general health began to deteriorate rapidly. The problem became so severe that he was placed in a nursing home at Harrogate for treatment and rest. This released Rosa from the nursing role she had for her father, but added the responsibility of travelling to see him at the home almost on a nightly basis. On the 6th of October 1948 at the age of eighty-four, Granda George Sunter died and was laid to rest in Gunnerside cemetery.

In the immediate post war period, work went on more or less as it had during the war as the reconstruction and rebuilding of bomb shattered towns and cities began in earnest. As that rebuilding began, there was a relative expansion in both vehicles and manpower, and a new era was dawning which was to transform Sunter Brothers, from a local road haulage company into a mover of some of the heaviest, highest and longest loads ever to be seen on the roads of the UK, but this was some years away. Part of that build up was the delivery of tanks (armoured) to various locations around the country. Drivers John Robinson and Phil Braithwaite carried the new Centurion battle tank from Vickers of Newcastle and on occasions delivered wartime tanks to the docks of Hull or for scrap to some of the many scrap metal businesses that had been created after the war.

One of the advantages of running a haulage business during the war had been that due to the important nature of road transport, long serving staff drivers such as John Robinson, Philip Braithwaite and Les Taylor had been exempt military service. This gave an advantage to Sunters, as there was a nucleus of experienced men already in place ready for the expected surge in post-war work. One new member of the staff who arrived in 1948 who did serve in the war was Joe Taylor. who had served in the Green Howards and had been evacuated out of Dunkirk. He then went to the Middle East and after seeing yet more action there, was given a job as a clerk in the battalions HQ. While being employed at the HQ, Joe took to paperwork as if born to it. His arrival at Sunters gave the company a man who was a great organiser and knew the 'In and Out' trays backwards and eventually ended up running the administrative side of the company. It was said, 'If it was OK by Joe Taylor it was usually OK by the bosses'

With the dawn of the 1950s and through an Act of Parliament, came the full force of the expected Nationalisation of the road transport industry. All what was described as normal road transport, i.e. light delivery vehicles and such were to be subsumed into the newly created British Road Services (BRS) All heavy mover companies were in theory, to be kept free from government control but in practice it didn't work out that way. Pickfords was owned by four rail companies and as the railways were within the public sector remit, so went the whole of Pickford's fleet. A concession was made for some heavy tractor units to be free from control, those which moved abnormal indivisible loads, e.g. loads that could not be carried in separate sections. However in reality the take over was almost total, causing great problems for the efficiency of the British haulage industry. Like all other road hauliers, Sunters was enveloped into BRS and as such suffered an initial decline as did many other small operators, but expansion was still their aim.

Shortly after the war, the National Service Bill was passed by Act of Parliament. All males between the age of eighteen and thirty years were to be eligible for conscription into one of Her Majesty's Armed Services for a period of eighteen months (later extended to two years with the outbreak of war in Korea). Due to National Service the armed forces expanded dramatically after the rapid demobilisation of wartime service personnel. This event was a lifeline for Tom Sunter ever the one to spot an opportunity for business. He realised that with thousands of servicemen passing through Catterick Camp, there would be a need to ferry them to the major towns and cities whenever they were allowed leave. This led to another diversification by Sunter Brothers Ltd.

Broadway Coaches & Taxi Cabs.

With introduction of National Service huge numbers of troops serving their two years of service were passing through Catterick camp on a regular basis. At the very outset it was obvious that some form of transport was going to be needed to carry them when ever leave was granted. To this end Tom purchased a fleet of twenty-two coaches, a Rolls Royce hearse, a mourners car plus four pre-war saloon taxis. The coaches were bought from all over the north-east and the taxi company was purchased from•Mark Oliver a former Canadian Army Captain who had married a local girl and set up the taxi business within Catterick camp (Now Catterick Garrison). The head quarters for the taxi company was in Shute Road on the camp. At about the same time Joss and Tom purchased Emile's hairdressing salon and Olga, Len's daughter and Margaret, Audrey's daughter ran the business for many years. Tom had to think of a name for his coach fleet and was discussing the subject with a chap called Winstanley who suggested the composite name of Sun-Win Coaches, utilising the first three letter of each name. Almost at the same time, Ken Simpson who had been with the company for some time as a coach cum taxi driver suggested Broadway Coaches. Tom immediately agreed with that name and so Broadway Coaches it became. Winstanley never spoke to Ken Simpson again.

The military authorities asked for tenders for the task of ferrying troops and 'The Brothers' negotiated a contract to ferry troops from the camp to towns and cities in the north of England. Although Sunters owned the coach fleet, Ken Curle assisted by Joss Sunter managed the entire operations and it was they who built up that branch of the business to make it the success that it became. Having this large fleet of coaches and a sizeable number of heavy goods vehicles, there was a relative increase in the staff both at the depot and at Catterick. To all the staff, the two Sunter brothers were never known or addressed neither as Tom or Len nor as Mr Sunter, a compromise was struck, they were known as Mr Tom and Mr Len and of course Joseph was always known as Joss.

The fleet of coaches was a mixed bag with an AEC, Guy, Foden and a Bedford, with one ancient petrol engined Thornycroft, which was eventually donated by Tom to Gunnerside football team as their coach for travelling to away matches. The fleet was later increased with the addition of a Leyland that was fitted with a Beccles body. This oddly shaped coach could reach speeds in excess of 70 mph, which was quite something in those early days. Within a very short time the fleet was fully occupied each weekend taking soldiers home for their thirty-six hour passes with the occasional forty-eight hour pass at the end of each month.

It is well known that soldiers everywhere always appear to be laden down with a whole plethora of kit-bags, packs and cases, even when going home for just a few hours. Catterick Camp covers hundreds of acres and it was almost impossible for the troops to get to the coach parks without help. That is when the fleet of taxis came into use.

Ann Percival
wife of
George and Friends

Phil Braithwaite,
Les Taylor, Denis Bevins

Paul Bateson standing next to Sunter's Coaches

Tom's wife Margaret and Joss's wife Audrey along with Rosa were occasionally pressed into service as taxi drivers. Their job was to drive to the various barracks on that sprawling military base, collect the troops and their luggage then take them to the coach park at Ypres Square. Sometimes a soldier who did not have a weekend pass would approach them and would plead with girls to be taken to the coach park. The soldier would be bundled into the boot of the taxi and taken to the coach where he would then be smuggled aboard. Facing the wrath of his sergeant major was to be the problem of the soldier on his return. On one occasion a soldier missed his particular coach and was visibly upset at losing his weekend at home. Without delay, Tom ushered the soldier into his car and followed the route the coach was taking for the soldier's hometown. He caught up with the bus some twenty miles away, flagged it down and the soldier got his weekend away. A generous gesture by any standards. Margaret Sunter recalls that the young men in uniform they ferried in the taxis were a cheerful but cheeky lot and would make ribald remarks to their female drivers, but they got back as good as they gave says Margaret. Some of the more daring young men even propositioned the two girls. It was all done in good fun says Margaret, but young men kept in barracks day in day out and without female company, there is no doubt that given half a chance.......

There was another taxi driver involved in the coaching operations and that was a young Aberdonian by the name of Murray (Jock) Fraser. Jock as he was known, was a serving soldier with the Royal Signals at Catterick and in his spare time drove a taxi for Ken Curle. When Jock reached his twenty-first birthday, Tom Sunter organised a PSV driving test for him even though he was still in the army. Jock passed the test with ease and was taken on as a part time coach driver taking troops home. No sooner had Corporal Fraser got used to his spare time activities, he was posted to Korea. Before he sailed Tom Sunter told him that when he finally left the army, there would be a job waiting for him at Northallerton. Jock arrived in that war torn peninsula in early 1952 and as a trained signals paratrooper attached to the Parachute Regiment, he saw a lot of action against the Chinese at the Imjin River with the Black Watch. In between breaks from the fighting the Chinese in the front line, he managed to do some controlled fighting in the rear by becoming the Army middleweight boxing champion. On returning to England and leaving the army, Jock went to see Tom about that promised job and was set to work driving the coaches and acting as mate to John Robinson on long distance haulage runs. Eventually becoming one of the company's large tractor unit drivers.

At about the same time as the arrival of Jock Fraser, a young boy by the name of George Sunter Percival also started his first job with Sunter Brothers. George was the son of Arthur and Isabel (Sunter) Percival and therefore the nephew of all the Sunter family. George began his working life as a yard boy doing odd jobs and helping out where and when he could. As soon as he was old enough he was taught to drive and began a long association with the company. Service with the RAF interrupted his work in the yard for three years, but on demobilisation he transferred to the coach branch of the company. He drove the coaches and was the official hearse driver whenever there was need. Later he was to act as unofficial chauffeur to

Tom, often driving the Rolls Royce and became the official spare parts collector for the firm.

Below is a sample prices charged for some of the destinations covered by Broadway Coaches when transporting troops.

Preston 16/9d, Lancaster 11/-, Hull 17/-, Manchester 16/9d, York 8/9d, Sheffield 16/9d Halifax 11/- Barnsley 15/- Liverpool £1.2s 3d.

All destinations were in the north, east and west. Other coach operators ferried troops from other military bases in other parts of the country. All the established drivers drove the coaches, and all have what might be termed as annoying stories about the times they were carrying out their duties as coach drivers. John Robinson recalls the time he took an army rugby XV to London for an inter-services match. The trip involved an overnight stay and he duly arrived and dropped the players off at a certain point with the strict instructions that they all meet the coach at that same point in the early morning. Once again, rugby players and soldiers being what they are, a great many of them were not at the pick-up point at the appointed time. By mid-day the missing players duly arrived bleary eyed, all down to a heavy drinking session and a liaison with a 'Lady of the night'. John could understand the motives of the young men, but it made him that much later for his return. One ruse worked out by the drivers was to pick up extra passengers whenever they could, and hopefully pocket the proceeds. Joss Sunter got wind of their activities and would 'ambush' a coach whenever it was approaching Catterick. He would wait in a gateway at the road side then step out in front of the coach and wave it down to ask if there were any more passengers aboard. A quick count would prove it; he then demanded the extra fares from the driver. Joss was attempting to recoup the company's money, which would have ended up in the driver's pocket. These escapdes led to a cat and mouse game between Joss and the errant coach drivers. Whenever nearing Catterick they would take a diversion to outwit his ambush. This eventually escalted into a near farce with Joss driving to the main pick up point for the many troops in Manchester, to check that passenger numbers on the coaches were as planned and that the drivers were sticking to the rules and weren't trying to make a few shillings on the side.

Ferrying troops was not the only business in which Sunter's Coaches were engaged; there were the usual seaside trips and outings for a whole variety of clubs and associations. Seaside and holiday resorts were in great demand after the war and as a result the Sunter fleet of coaches was kept extremely busy with the demands for trips to the coast and other places of interest. This was good news for the company and for Joss Sunter, but it wasn't such good news for the drivers. Long wearying hours away from home taking coach loads of mothers, fathers and not a few noisy children to such locations as Blackpool, Morcambe and Scarborough almost day after day became the norm. Then on completion of the trip, the coach had to be cleaned. It must be remembered that the heavy drivers John Robinson, Phil Braithwaite and Les Taylor also had to double up as coach drivers at weekends. The constant long hours away from home was to play havoc with their health, to say nothing of the loneliness suffered by their wives and children. The standard pay for driving a coach was £1 per day with the possibility of a couple of bob in tips. Phil Braithwaite recalls an incident that led to a clash between him and Mr. Tom, all down

Racing at Redcar Sands

The Jaguar XK 120 GVN 1

The Mercedes Gullwing

At a carnival in Gunnerside,
Tom is the 'Bride' William Calvert a local builder is the 'Groom'

to the long hours of coach driving. Phil had done four consecutive coach trips from the Thursday to the Sunday inclusive, arriving back in the early hours of the Monday morning. He didn't stir from his bed until mid-day and managed to get to the depot just before 1 o'clock. He stopped to speak to one of the other drivers and was confronted by Tom Sunter who told him that he was going to have 10/- docked from his wages for being late. By then Phil had had enough. He put on his jacket and told Tom that he was leaving the job there and then and stormed off. When Tom realised that Phil had hardly slept for the past few days, he relented and called Phil back, apologised and withdrew the threat of the ten bob reduction. That was just one of many altercations the drivers had with Mr.Tom and Mr.Len Sunter. To be fair to both brothers, they were always being faced by bogus claims for hours worked and expenses and at times staff who would occasionally try to pull a fast one.

A large fleet of coaches not only required mechanical maintenance but also cleaning and interior décor. Audrey Sunter was given the task of making seat covers for several of the coaches, a job that she initially took up with enthusiasm. After many laborious hours of stitching and sewing she completed almost a hundred loose seat covers for three of the coaches. Quite an achievement for someone who was not a trained seamstress. George Percival's wife Ann likewise helped with the interior maintenance of the coaches, Her task was to clean up the detritus after each boozy trip or soldierly week-end, and one can only imagine what that entailed. Once the rubbish had been cleared the whole coach had to be washed and the windows

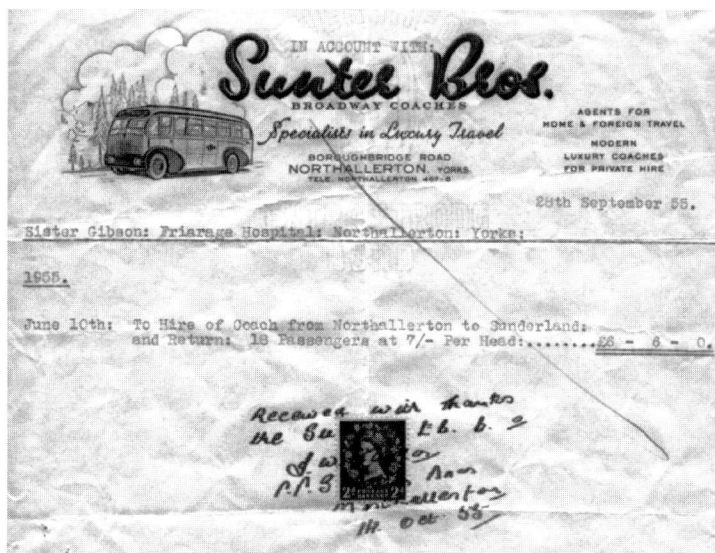

A receipt for a Sunter's Coach ordered by Sister Gibson of the Friarage Hospital Northallerton.

cleaned, all done for free in the interests of the firm. Sometime later Sunters bought out a rival company Scott's Greys, a well established coaching firm with a fleet of up to date coaches.

Not only did the brothers run the coaching and taxi businesses; they were also funeral directors. Along with the taxis and coaches, they purchased a Humber Pullman hearse and a mourner's car. One well known character who helped to run the undertaking business was Geoff Whetherhill who was later to be a leading undertaker in Northallerton. In the year of 1958 a young seventeen year old youth, Roy Pickard began his apprenticeship with Sunters coaches. Roy was to move to Northallerton and stay with the company almost thirty years. Both he and Piechochi along with another apprentice David Murphy were to be the mainstay of the maintenance staff for the company.

Although the coaching, taxi and undertaking businesses was an important aspect of Sunters Ltd, it was the heavy haulage business that occupied Tom and Len's time. The number of staff employed had grown steadily, and as business contracts grew so did the wages bill. Wages in those early days were always paid in pounds shillings and pence in a standard pay packet issued on a certain day of the week, usually a Friday. For a fairly large company such as Sunters with more than a hundred staff to pay, making up the wages was a time consuming and delicate business as no one likes being paid short. Being paid over was a different argument. However Arthur Port wages clerk was up to the job. There is one story of Joe Taylor that seems to show the ethos of the times. All the staff at Sunters were paid on a Friday and of course they were paid in cash. After Arthur Port had made up the wages, Joe would hand out the pay packets to whoever was in the depot at the time. Any staff who were on the road or away, he would endeavour to pay at a later date. That later date was usually in 'Sunter's pub' The Station Hotel or later the Harewood Arms in Northallerton. Joe would pack all the unclaimed pay packets into a Gladstone Bag and take it to the pub the following day. As he played dominoes, the Gladstone Bag was placed 'safely' under the table. As the men arrived in the pub he would hand out the pay packets. Apart from the fact that people are paid differently today, carrying such an enormous amount of money on ones person would surely have brought trouble.

The reader may gather that when it came down to cars, Tom had always valued simplicity, boldness, quality, and durability. This is probably true and it was at this time that he had become almost impassioned with the engineering characteristics embodied in the pre thirties three litre and four and a half litre Bentleys. Over a four year period during the war he acquired a series of three of those cars and thoroughly enjoyed the handling as well as the torque and long stroke that provided power and top gear flexibility as well as the exhaust note which was music to the motor enthusiast's ear. In 1946 his brother George told him of a Lagonda belonging to a Director of Saxone Shoes that was for sale as it had lain idle for several years and was covered in dust. When the car was washed off a beautifully styled two-tone green four door saloon with exotic features including a glass sliding roof with blind and a chromium dashboard was revealed. Tom was immediately enamoured with the car and bought it. In spite of the V12 engine configuration it did not develop the expected power that Tom had hoped and he openly said that W.O. Bentley was mistaken in thinking he could design anything. In 1947 there was a flood of ex army vehicles on the market and Tom was tempted to purchase an ex US Army Ford/Willys Jeep. It was a fundamentally simple, robust and extremely versatile four-wheel drive vehicle, which could cope with almost any terrain and Tom, found trekking through the heather such a delightful pastime

The purchase of vehicles and sports cars in particular continued. In 1948 a new Jaguar sports car was launched and this hit the motor world with a resounding impact in its every feature. It was the spectacular Jaguar XKl20. Tom immediately realised that the car was a world-beater. Demand for this sensational car was overwhelming and even George Sunter and his association with Jaguar, took until 1951 before he could obtain the first delivery to his company. George incurred some backlash from his own Company for selling it to Tom, even though it had been ordered from the time it was on the drawing board. With motor racing now in his blood, he had the XK fully modified for racing at the factory. He employed a racing engineer to keep it performance tuned and raced it on Coatham and Saltburn sands against such opposition as Keith Schellengburg a former British Bob Sleigh champion. The Flamboyant Schellengburg drove his 8 litre Bentley to whom Tom had to forfeit a handicap. Tom achieved the fastest speed trial ever of 117mph and the record still stands to this day. He also drove the Jaguar XK at Croft, Turnbury and Berwick and recorded several wins including one against the redoubtable Stirling Moss. The above shows that Tom liked speed, but speed under control. Legend has it that he had a notice pinned in his Jag XK120 to the effect that passengers should ensure that the door is securely fastened as it has a tendency to fly open at speeds above 120mph. This is probably apocryphal but somehow typical.

From time to time the diabetes would bring home to Tom the dangers of neglecting his insulin regime. Ken Simpson who had left the employ of Sunters several years earlier to take a post as a civilian army driver at Catterick Camp recalls an incident that is as vivid today as it was when it happened. It was while Ken was out with a body of troops on the moors in a truck that he was instrumental in what can be quite safely described as saving Tom Sunter's life. Tom's problem with diabetes never became less than severe, but he refused to let it rule his life. He had been injecting himself daily with insulin since those dark days when he almost died of the disease. It must be said that Tom followed his insulin regime with reasonable discipline and cleaned the needles-occasionally, and learned to inject himself when he felt the need and not follow a strict regime, but there were the occasional lapses The day Ken was on the moors, he spotted a blue Bentley pulled in by the side of the road and recognised it and the driver, Tom Sunter. Tom was sat staring straight ahead as though in a trance. Ken stopped went over to the car and spoke to Tom asking him if he was OK, realising that he may be having a problem. Tom mumbled and motioned for Ken to go to the glove compartment and get out the hypodermic syringe and insulin. This he did whereupon Tom injected himself with insulin and began to recover. He thanked Ken briefly for his help, but finished with a warning. Tom told him quite strongly that under no circumstances must he tell his sister Rosa! Obviously he knew that Rosa would berate him mercilessly if ever she found out, as she kept a strict eye on his diabetic medication. Although Rosa was the youngest of the Sunter children, she acted like a big sister to Tom. For Ken there was not so much as another thank you for his timely help and the episode was never mentioned ever again even when Ken became an employee of Tom's once more some years later.   Ken is philosophical about the incident, and is just pleased that he happened to be there and was able to help his old boss. It was surely fate that decided that Ken Simpson was passing that part of the moors road that day. It is fair to say that any other person may well have ignored the car and driver and carried on with their journey.

Another classic car, which punctuated Tom's motoring life story, was one that he immediately recognised as another world leader when it was introduced in 1954. The car in question, was truly exceptional in having the first structural space frame design, and the first fuel injection engine in a sports production car, an inclined engine block for lower centre of gravity, superb body styling with overhead hinged doors, that is the doors opened upwards and outwards in the shape of a wing. This car was of course, the Mercedes-Benz 300SL Gullwing. The power and handling performance was exceptional but the brakes barely matched the power and speed, and Tom said that it was therefore so important to drive on the speedometer. Into today's jargon, it could 'Go' but it could hardly 'Stop'. The access road to his later home, Spring End, overlooking Gunnerside, was a mile incline along the hillside and his nephew Malcolm White recalls that once as a passenger in the Gullwing on that run was a stirring, ecstatic experience, which gave immense confidence in Tom's driving skills.

Tom Sunter although generally a good employer and of a generous nature even if short of temper at times, one aspect of being an employer he could not countenance and that was Trade Unionism, the Trade Union movement was anathema to him. Sometime after the war when a trade union was being established at Sunters, an area union representative of the Transport and General Workers Union visited the yard to speak to Les Taylor. Tom immediately ordered the man off his premises and told him that if he wished to speak to any of his employees, he had to speak to them on the roadside out of the yard. Eventually Tom had to face the facts. Many sites to where his men delivered were union controlled and any driver without a union card was simply refused admission. Mysteriously Tom procured a 'union card' and would issue it to his staff, which got them onto the site for their deliveries. Tom Sunter was a man of the old order and boss/employee relationship change did not come easily to him. It must be remembered that at the time when Tom Sunter was anti union it was also the time when the trade unions appeared to have a grip of the country with a series of devastating strikes. He would not allow any member of his staff to be a member of any union until legislation compelled him to recognise that he was fighting a losing battle and Sunters had a union rep and many members. With the co-operation of the Union an attempt was made to introduce a Pension and Life Assurance Scheme for the workforce. After somewhat of a delayed start, the Life Assurance Scheme brought out by Sunter Brothers was an honest and reasonable effort and to make the company a modern employer the scheme got off the ground. Although it ran well for a number of years, but due to it not being properly thought out and being linked to the rise in the cost of living, it withered on the vine, lost its value and was finally scrapped.

The Saga of Bradwell and...Rotinoff.

In the early 1950s, Sunters was becoming a force to be reckoned with in the heavy haulage industry, but still lacked truly heavyweight tractor units or a contract that would give them a chance to compete in the heavy league. With the election of a Conservative government, the nationalisation of the road haulage industry was repealed thus freeing the big companies to expand. In 1953, Sunter Brothers received £130,000 from the government in compensation for the nationalisation of their company, from that time; the brothers began to build up their fleet with the purchase of several heavy tractors and articulated units. Despite the upgrading with modern vehicles, they still ran a chain driven Scammel that was slightly long in the tooth for the loads that it was required to haul, but still had its uses. The impetus to increase and improve the fleet was due to the fierce competition of such heavyweights as Pickfords and Wynns who still dominated the heavy market. Tom Sunter was determined that his company would one day compete with the biggest and the best. With the freeing from government control of the nation's transport, the two brothers purchased their first new vehicle since before the war, the first of four to be bought within a space of five years. All were initially handed over to senior driver, John Robinson. It is worth highlighting the basic pros and cons of this vehicle as it had its own vices and virtues. The 4x4 Scammel Mountaineer, registered number-KVN 604, powered by a Meadows engine was the first postwar purchase by Sunters. The Mountaineer was officially limited to draw 45 tons but like almost every operator, Sunters tried to get their new acquisition to draw far in excess of that rating. The Meadows engine was somewhat underpowered and when it was attempting a steepish hill, it was not uncommon for the driver to hail a passing 'eight legger' (eight-wheeled lorry) and beg a push. which usually cost the begging driver

John Robinson delivering the first load with Scammell Mountaineer KVN604

five bob for the 'hire'. The haulage companies considered this sort of 'hired help' normal practice on the open road. The trailer that complemented the Mountaineer, a sixty-ton Crane float, became somewhat of a nightmare for John Robinson and the gangs that had to work with it. Each time a consignment needed to be loaded or unloaded, the rear axles complete with their huge wheels and tyres had to be knocked out and then replaced. To add to their discomfiture, the trailer had a tendency to snake while on the move, it was however an excellent speed restrictor.

The next tractor unit was a Gardner powered 6x4 reg. number PPY 264 that turned out to be a vast improvement on the pulling power of the Mountaineer, but for this, it forfeited speed and was extremely slow. It could conquer hills with ease by the use of hand operated reduction hubs turned into a low-range setting. The method for altering the reduction hubs was by the insertion of a small tommy bar into the hub ring and then ratcheting the hub round to the desired setting, however, this had the effect of reducing the tractor to a road speed of 16mph-max! With the low speed and the high revving engine, the temperature in the cab of the ancient Foden often soared to almost unbearable levels.

The year of 1955 saw the arrival of the third tractor to the company, a 6x6 Scammel Constructor-NAJ 920. The Constructor was a superb vehicle even if the engine tended to bellow somewhat inside the cab, but the 12 speed gearbox made the tractor extremely versatile, but it needed some leg muscle power to operate the clutch pedal. The purchasing of the next tractor is alluded to in later pages. At this juncture it is worth remembering that the greater part of Sunter haulage was carried out by the company's fleet of articulated vehicles and artic drivers of which there were many. These were a mixture of Foden, Atkinson, AEC, Guys and Leyland prime movers with one special International.

In the years of 1957 and 1958 there were three major events that in various ways affected Sunter Brothers. The first was the purchasing of the heavy haulage company of Crook and Willington of Bishop Auckland in County Durham. This strengthened Sunter's arm considerably with the addition of several vehicles that included two of the famous American Diamond 'T' VPT 85 and TUP 5. The 'T' heavy transporters originally brought over by the Americans during the war and were generally used for transporting tanks and armoured vehicles and proved excellent for the job so much so that many haulage companies in the UK made great use of it when they became available after the war despite it being left hand drive. The Diamond T had a 176 bhp engine ably assisted by a 12 speed gearbox. It could and did quite easily pull well in excess of that rating. If the 'T' had a drawback it was its cramped cab and poorly positioned headlights, but the brace brought from Crook and Willington were a great asset to the company.

Not only did Sunters acquire more vehicles with the purchase of Crook and Willington, which included a two-stroke Foden complete with two gear levers; they also acquired top driver Tony Swann. Tony was a diffident easygoing man who apparently always wore a collar and tie whenever he was driving and this was long before anyone had heard the name Eddie Stobart. Tony was the only one who could drive the 2 strokes Foden with any degree of skill. He would operate both gear levers simultaneously while blithely leaving the steering to go it's own way. Jock Fraser tried to master the old Foden, but gave up after managing to get just two gears and as he put it they were first and neutral! With Tony Swann came a large uncompromising character by the name of John Easton. Of gypsy lineage John was to become one of the most experienced mates and Black Gang member of the company, and he was known to stand no nonsense when his mind was set.

With the requisitioning of this company, which temporarily operated out of Bishop Auckland, Tom Sunter like all road haulage proprietors had to justify why he needed the A, B, and C heavy goods vehicle licenses for his business. Buying vehicles already licensed no matter the mechanical state of repair of the vehicle made good business sense as the licence went with the vehicle. To acquire a licence, representations had to be made in a special court. Normally, solicitors carried out such work, but Tom Sunter undertook to represent the company himself. Although having only a basic education, therefore being an unlettered man, he took up studying the procedures for putting forward such a case in a court. He even studied and scanned the Oxford English dictionary in a search for the correct words. He didn't simply learn the words parrot fashion or for affectation, he learnt them to understand how he might use the words in the proper context and how to make them flow in conversation. All this stood him in good stead when he presented his case to the courts at Newcastle. Such was the determination of Tom Sunter.

The second event to affect the firm was the death at forty-nine of Joss Sunter the youngest of the four Sunter brothers. Joss had been suffering from lung cancer for quite some time and on the 27th August of 1957 he succumbed to the disease. He was laid to rest alongside his mother and father in Gunnerside cemetery.

The third event of that year and the most far reaching in the terms of business was the winning of a huge and prestigious heavy hauling contract. From the end of the war, the British Nuclear Industry had been evolving rapidly and nuclear power was being trumpeted as the energy of the future. To this end the Central Electricity Authority, was planning to build several nuclear power stations across the country. The first of these power stations was to be built on the Blackwater Estuary at Bradwell in Essex. It is fair to say that the siting of the power station was the easy part of the planning. It was one thing to build the station; it was another installing all the various internal plant. Without question, the greatest problem was to be the transporting of some of that plant from Tees-side to Bradwell.

In 1956 Head Wrightson Heavy Construction Company based at Thornaby and Stockton had been given a contract to design, build and fabricate twelve heat exchange vessels for that nuclear power station. The building of those vessels was to a standard never expected, asked or achieved previously. They had to be so designed as to give a guaranteed trouble free service throughout the life of each vessel. Head Wrightson achieved all of those aims in the design and construction of the vessels, but there was still the question of how they were to be transported to the site. The dimensions of each vessel were; 92ft 4 ins high, 20ft in diameter and a weight of 238 tons. Put another way that was relevant to road transportation, they were 92ft 4 ins long, 20ft wide and 20 ft high. It had been realised throughout the building of the vessels, that transportation by road or rail was out of the question. Due to the limitations of normal means of delivery, the vessels were so designed to facilitate ocean towage. Head Wrightson's engineers built scale models of the vessels and tested them for their buoyancy and just as importantly to check for possible water damage. Uniquely, each vessel was constructed with a false keel for stability while travelling the North Sea. The trials were a success and the go ahead was given for the preparing of the full size vessels.

By the end of 1957 the first of the twelve heat exchange units was nearing completion and a contract to heavy haulage companies to tender for the task of transporting them was sent out. The leading heavy company that had the capability and capacity to do the job, namely, Pickfords, was expected to get the job. At that time Pickfords was still under the control of BRS and as such, a manager who would have to go through his chain of command as it were, to reach a decision ran each of their depots. Added to Pickford's refusal to take on the contract was their reluctance to have their trailer units submerged in the seawater, which is what was to happen to their trailer units as part of the move. Head Wrightson did not have the time for a long drawn out saga of decision making and so listened very intently to Tom Sunter who had applied for the contract. They accepted his representations that his company was able to carry out the task, which, considering, that at the time, his company did not have the wherewithal to do the job, showed the quality and tenacity of his negotiating prowess. It was said of Tom Sunter, that he saw solutions before he saw problems, and his negotiating for the Bradwell contract seemed to confirm this. A successful outcome to the securing of that contract could not hide the fact that Sunter Brothers did not have the heavy trailer configuration with which to carry those monstrous units but they did have adequate tractor units. This did not faze Tom one little bit. Without delay he paid a visit to Cranes the leading trailer company in the UK to negotiate a contract for the building of a new type of multi wheeled trailer unit that could carry the proposed loads to the nuclear power station. Eventually 2x100 ton Crane bogies were purchased, and that was problem number one solved. Although Sunters had an array of reasonably heavy tractor units, none had the capability to haul the proposed weight of the heat exchange units each weighing in at 238 tons, and that was problem number two. So his next visit was to a small motor engineering factory near Slough and to speak to the owner and senior engineer, a certain George Rotinoff.

George Rotinoff, a highly qualified engineer, was born in Russia but was brought over to England by his parents when he was just two years old. Heavy tractor units were his speciality and his current project was a 6x4 ballasted tractor powered by a Rolls Royce engine. Ballast was several heavy metal castings placed on heavy tractor units to act as a counter weight for the rear of the vehicle. This weight was needed to keep pressure on the rear driving wheels when hauling heavy loads.

Rotinoff's basic design for his latest model was similar in looks at least, to the American Diamond T980 but developed more power, had a superior gearbox (in terms of servicing) better cab refinements having sliding cab doors, and greater dimensions. It was a motor engineer's dream when it came to working on the gearbox. This had an unboltable flat plate on the top of the gear box housing which allowed the lay shafts to be slotted in and out by hand. The cab could be removed (by crane) to facilitate working on the engine. Although the idea of a removable cab was probably a first, George Rotinoff did not think of siting a set of lifting lugs on the corners of the cab for the crane to do the lifting. For this job, a batten of timber had to be passed through the cab windows with a rope attached to the batten. This rather clumsy method of removing the cab took the edge off what was basically a sound idea. From the point of view of the auto electricians, the Rotinoff was perfect. All wiring to the various services was threaded through a series of looms with multi pins plugs and connecting sockets. Hours of servicing were saved by these simple but effective innovations.

The Rotinoff Atlantic was the vehicle that was being currently designed, built and tested at the factory, and that was the tractor unit Tom had in mind for the Bradwell move. For the first boiler to be moved at Bradwell, George Rotinoff was preparing three of his Atlantics accompanied by a great deal of photographic and film publicity. Sunter Brothers were to eventually purchase one Rotinoff Atlantic, the only heavy haulage company to do so in the UK. They were never to regret it.

By the spring of 1958 everything was in place for the start of what was to be the largest and heaviest load ever moved in the UK. Head Wrightson had hired a sea going tug, the SS 'Fiery Cross' to tow the first of the boilers from Tees-side, along the North Sea to the Blackwater Estuary in Essex. Special wooden jetties had been constructed to take the boilers from the water on to a concrete causeway rising from the sea. The principle was that the Crane bogies would rest in the water at the position the boilers were to be placed. The boilers were to be floated and anchored down by cables to await the ebbing tide. As the tide receded, the boilers would settle onto the trailers. In the meantime, the trailers had been placed in the water for some considerable time for the task. To counter the seepage of seawater into the braking system of the trailers, members of Sunter's Machinery Installation Team, aka-The Black Gang had packed the exteriors of the hubs with water-resistant grease. In the event, the seawater won, the brakes on the trailer were totally useless. The Black Gang of Sunters was a squad of men employed specifically to help prepare loads for moving to their destination. They then would help to unload and prepare it to be moved into position on the site. Once off the trailer they would then manoeuvre the load by the use of jacks, crowbars, and rollers to say nothing of a whole lot of cursing and sweat. As the day of the move approached, Sunters personnel arrived with all that was necessary to make the move and with a lot that was unnecessary.

George Rotinoff arrived at Bradwell with three of his Atlantics, which were to carry out the first pull, all three being differing models. The two to join Sunter's Rotinoff had double driving wheels and with different axle ratios and gearboxes.

The Mighty Rotinoff

*The first Bradwell boiler ready for
the pull up the incline.
Three differing models of the
Rotinoffs were utilised.
George Rofinoff
is the man in the raincoat.*

*The moving of the boilers by three of
Sunter's tractors. The pioneer (coffee pot)
heads up the Constructor
and the Rotinoff.*

*Jock Fraser guiding John Robinson
at Bradwell.*

Peter Clemmet easing the Rotinoff down Linthorpe Road, Middlesbrough.
John Robinson is riding shotgun.

Jock Fraser reversing the 'Rot' whilst standing on the running board as it heads up the
Super Constructor and a 168 ton x 148ft load in the Shell oil terminal Teesport.

John Robinson, the senior driver for Sunters who had been designated the role of driving a Rotinoff, had arrived at the site some days earlier. He was preparing the detail for the great pull and it cannot be stressed enough that what was being attempted was a very great undertaking indeed and a first in the history of heavy haulage.

The concrete causeway built for the towing of the boilers started with an initial gradient of 1-in-10 and the pull had to be undertaken from a standing start. A move that needed great consideration and timing. John had been in 'training' for a few days, dragging a wheeled barge around on dry land so that he could get used to the sort of resistance the monster boiler's weight might give, and to get used to the Rotinoff Atlantic, especially the gear box. Came the day for the Bradwell big pull, and everything was in place. The trailers had been lowered into the water; the boiler had been settled on to the trailers and secured. The weather was fine and it was the moment of truth for all concerned, Sunters, Rotinoff and not least Head Wrightson. Without doubt the reputations of both Sunters and Rotionff lay with this contract, as failure would have meant complete ruin for both. The three Rotinoff tractor units were reversed into position with John Robinson at the controls of the third unit connected to the trailers. The two others driven by Rotinoff drivers were headed up. (Three tractors in-line ahead of the load.). George Rotinoff was there with Tom Sunter and both were running around and fussing ensuring that everything was in place and set up. George was to be the sole controller of the vehicles in this particular haul out. When everything was ready, he advised each driver to start their engines and reach a designated number of RPM on their dashboard rev counters. When this was attained and the drivers were to indicate as such, while Tom Sunter was ready with a downbeat of a white handkerchief in his hand, to signal the start of the pull. It must be remembered that this huge load of 238 tons was being hauled from a standing start up a 1-in-10 gradient. All three tractors were fitted with manual gearboxes and co-ordination of clutch control by all three drivers was absolutely crucial to the success of the project. A single second's delay by one or the other could have resulted in broken half shafts, leaving the whole load stranded in the water. An unthinkable situation. As each driver indicated that he had attained the required RPM, came the vital moment. With a flourish of the white handkerchief, Tom lowered his right arm. With a rumbling roar, three Rotinoff Atlantics inched smoothly forward with their gigantic load and with consummate ease hauled the boiler up the incline on to the level ground. The first of many phases was completed. As soon as the three Rotinoffs and the load had reached level ground, the first two were unhitched and John Robinson pulled the load to the power station in his solo tractor. The operation went a great deal more smoothly than was expected, but there were just a couple of hiccups on the way. As John negotiated a fairly sharp bend the front of the boiler protruded out by almost 45 degrees and took several tiles and bricks off a nearby house. Tom Sunter, who was in overall charge, was guiding and cajoling John to the site and walked in front giving directions. On more than one occasion John had to ignore Tom's signals, as his experience told him that the tractor and the load would not respond to that direction. Tom as ever, gave way to that experience. The reason for Tom Sunter misguiding John was probably due to the deterioration in his eyesight due to the diabetes. It was found later that Tom had a reduction in his stereoscopic vision, which affected his judgement and perception. Added to those problems, it must be remembered that the trailer bogies that were bearing the weight of the boiler, were of a hundred ton capacity, and the boiler weighed 238 tons, which meant that the trailers were running twenty percent over weight, unthinkable now in today's climate of Health and Safety and paperwork!

Over the next fourteen months, the remaining eleven heat exchange boilers were towed by sea and hauled in exactly the same manner to Bradwell except that there was only one Rotinoff in the train of tractors being used; two resident Sunter tractors gave the extra pull. John Robinson was to tow each one of the boilers onto the site bar the last. En-route to Bradwell in the redoubtable Rotinoff for the last boiler unit, the gearbox overheated and seized up leaving John stranded in Cheshire. The eleven further pulls with drivers Jock Fraser, Jack Thompson and Jack Emms taking part, generated next to no publicity, it had all been garnered in that first historic effort. On one of those occasions, Tom's wife Margaret and their two daughters Ann and Mallie were given a grandstand view when they travelled down to Bradwell and sat in one of the tractor units as it hauled the boiler out of the sea. Without doubt the Bradwell contract hoisted Sunter Brothers higher into the league of heavy haulage, where from that position they were able to challenge the mighty Pickfords and Wynns for super heavy contracts that were coming along due to the expansion in Britain's industries. From that time in 1957-58 Sunter Brothers never looked back. A great deal of the credit for this must go to Tom Sunter whose vision and willingness to take a chance was crucial.

Life has its constant ironies and road hauling industry was never short of them. A short time after all the boilers were installed and running at Bradwell, the boffins had designed and had built smaller, lighter and more efficient boilers that would do the same job, and in a short time all the original ones had been replaced. Nonetheless, this did not detract from Tom Sunter's vision and courage. The 'Bradwell move' was the acme of his career in heavy haulage.

Although Tom Sunter was heavily involved with the build up of the company and in particular with the delivery of the boilers to Bradwell in 1957 and 1958, he somehow still found time to stand and canvas for a seat on the Swaledale Parish Council. He duly won a resounding victory and was elected as the member for Reeth. His acceptance speech was recognised as electrifying in its delivery showing once again the command of public speaking that had been self-taught. Tom didn't bask in the glory of his election but set to work helping his constituents. One of his first successes for the local community was the laying of a footpath/pavement for Reeth village school, which until then was a muddy track along the road. Almost immediately he was given credit for the laying of another pathway to a local farm. It happened after Tom fell into conversation with a local farmer who complained that the roadway running to his farm track was in a bad state of repair and asked if anything could be done about it. Tom promised that he would look into it. The very next day the Council road workmen came along and repaired the roadway outside the farmer's track all part of the ongoing road repair system. When Tom and the farmer next met, the farmer couldn't thank Tom enough. Tom took the compliments but kept his counsel and the farmer was none the wiser at the sheer coincidence of it all.

For several years Tom had been experiencing some restriction of movement in both hands. It may be that he was becoming more aware of it when handling the steering wheel and gear lever of cars especially while motor racing. The condition was Dupuytrens contracture discovered in 1831 by a French surgeon, Baron Guillaume Dupuytren which is described in the Oxford English dictionary as, 'Fixed forward curvature of one or more fingers, caused by the growth of fibrous tissue' The complaint had a familial incidence as Tom's father had it in one hand. It is thought that one factor of the onset of the ailment is repeated trauma to the palm, perhaps by cranking engines in Tom's case, and the use of the horse's halter, reins and cart shafts in his father's case. It is seen more commonly in Australian males apparently due to their pioneering activity in the outback. It is usually most marked in the curving of ring and little fingers but can affect all digits. Surgery to correct it consists of carefully dissecting out the fibrous tissue from a jungle of delicate structures; a procedure fraught with risk. His nephew Malcolm White, a qualified anaesthetist, took him to see the world famous plastic surgeon, Anglo-New Zealander, Sir Archibald McIndoe famous for his treatment of fire scarred airmen in World War 11 at the famous Queen Victoria Hospital, East Grinstead. After the operation Tom's bandaged hands were suspended from stands as a routine measure to improve drainage and so aid healing. During recovery, he felt the onset of a diabetic attack and called the nurse who assured him that he had been given the correct amount of insulin. He recognised the symptoms only too readily and asked for the ward doctor who again reassured him, but Tom had the strength of conviction and said that he would need to pull down his hands unless his diabetic feeling was corrected. His obvious determination caused the staff to attend to the sugar imbalance and all was well. The operation eventually provided both an excellent functional and cosmetic result that allowed Tom to resume full control of his hands and his cars.

Having regained full hand and finger movement his next auto purchase was the ultimate in motorcars, a blue and silver Rolls Royce Silver Cloud bearing the very personal registration number of TS 123. Tom was well known for his generosity even if he could be a hard taskmaster. Shortly after acquiring the Rolls Royce he agreed to loan the car to Celia Fawcett who was to be married to Brian Coulthard. Celia who was a secretary in the offices at Boroughbridge Road depot had lost her father when she was a young girl and not only did Tom give her the use of the Rolls, he also acted as her surrogate father and 'gave her away' at the wedding ceremony. A typical friendly gesture. Although Tom enjoyed the refinements and qualities of the Rolls, he never flaunted them. This was his attitude with all his possessions, for he was a humble man by nature, and always rated presentation of importance without the accompanying snobbery. Similarly he often told his daughters to ever remember their origins and never to stretch themselves beyond those limits.

As a man who seemed to genuinely care for the people of the Dales, it seemed only natural that he became a notional candidate for Westminster politics. Major Dugdale the sitting Member of Parliament for Richmond suggested to Tom that he should consider standing as a parliamentary candidate as he thought he had the makings of an MP. This came to nought, as in the first instance Margaret did not want the problems of being an MP's wife and Tom would not have taken kindly to the travelling to London and all that being a politician entailed. Similarly the suggestion that he stand to become Mayor of Richmond came to nothing.

In 1960, another Sunter came on to the scene; this was Peter, the only son of Len and Sybil and the only male heir of the three Sunter brothers involved in the business. Peter Sunter who was born in 1942 stayed on at school to gain his 'A' levels

Tom Sunter's Rolls Royce TS 123
on wedding duty in the Dales.

Tom's Rolls on the wedding day of Celia
Fawcett and Brian Coulthard.
Tom 'gave Celia away'

and in particular studied history and geography hoping that having those levels might eventually lead to a job that involved both of those subjects. It was not to be. One Friday night a short time after leaving school for the last time, Peter was contemplating his working future and thinking on the lines his qualifications, his father came home from the yard and said in his usual blunt and forthright way, "You are starting work in the office at the yard on Monday" Peter's protestation were brushed aside even when his mother had tried to explain to her husband that it was Peter's life and choice. Despite a few harsh words between the three of them, nothing changed, 'you start on Monday' was the uncompromising reply and that was that.

However on starting work at the office on the Monday, it was to be no easy option via a cushy position in management with the company for Peter just because he was the nephew of the boss, for him it was learning from the ground up, only then could he hope for promotion. He began his working life with Sunter Brothers as an office boy and a driver's mate, learning through the nitty-gritty of life on the road and at first hand. Peter says that once he got over his disappointment he would not have had it any other way. He realised from early on that if he were ever to go into management it was imperative that he should have some idea of what it was like from every aspect of the job and from the point of view of the men in the yard. He does confess however, that although it was vital he learned the hard way, he still thought it extremely hard work.

Familiar Scenes.
Jock Fraser filling the north of Northallerton High Street with a Constructor and load.
Jock was not best pleased as it was New Years Eve.

John Robinson doing the same with the Rotinoff in South Parade with Jock Fraser
pushing with the 100 ton Foden. These four stalwarts arrived seven days early with this load.

A mighty line up.
The Rotinoff - Super Constructor - Constructor - Junior Constructor - Pioneer.

The 100 ton Foden heads up the Super Constructor with
the Mountaineer doing the pushing.
Village unknown.

Constructor 447 DPY
'at rest' outside the
Green Tree pub
in Yarm

*The Rotinoff
with a
Nicolas trailer
'Grounding'
while passing over
Layerthorpe Bridge,
York.*

*The Rotinoff
passing through
the Market Place
and then round the
sharp right angle
bend of the
Regent Cinema
at Thirsk*

*No. 44 Corporation Bus
in the wake of
Constructor 447DPY*

1963 - The year of change

The diabetes that afflicted Tom Sunter way back in the mid 1920s was now beginning to have a deleterious affect on his general health. First and foremost of those problems was the steady deterioration in his eyesight followed by a general loss of energy. With these ongoing health problems, Tom had already begun the process of putting up the business for sale. Tom was in his sixty-fourth year and Len was in his sixty-second year so both were nearing the age of retirement. Although Len had a son, Tom did not have a male heir to take over the company and he was considering selling the business. Tom's enjoyment of life and the challenge of business were slowly being restricted due to the deterioration of his eyesight brought about by his illness. Another factor was that the stalwart and lynch pin of the office Joe Taylor, was beginning to suffer ill health. Joe was the man who had the finger on the pulse of the company in terms of the running of the administration. Since 1957, Tom had suffered three left retinal haemorrhages and it was obvious that something had to be done to prevent a recurrence. His nephew Malcolm took him to see a diabetic specialist by the name of John Nabarro, brother of the Conservative M.P Sir Gerald Nabarro, who practised at the Middlesex Hospital. The specialist considered that Tom had controlled his diabetes remarkably well considering that he had suffered from the ailment for thirty-two years. This control had undoubtedly been due to his keen awareness of his insulin and sugar requirements during each day rather than abiding by a stipulated dosage. He was advised to reduce his driving to short distances and to delegate it as far as possible. This was when his nephew George Percival became his unofficial chauffeur for many of the long distances trips and for travel to local business meetings. When his nephew Peter passed his driving test, he too was called upon to drive his uncle to various places and put on route planning. Peter recalls how within just two days of his passing the driving test, he was sent with John Robinson to plan a route for a large load that was to be routed through the centre of London. John was an old hand at driving throughout the capital so for him it was nothing. They both arrived in the car at the rendezvous point with the Metropolitan police and the route was planned. They then repaired to the police canteen for a meal after which John became extremely ill and was unable to drive, so Peter who had almost no experience of driving had to take over the car driving and negotiate the centre of London and all the way back to Northallerton. He found it somewhat of an interesting experience. Thus was the introduction to the harsh competitive world of heavy transport for the young Sunter. Peter was also expected to help with the recovery of the inevitable breakdowns of the fleet and he recalls one in particular. The Fodens held by the company were inherently prone to throwing prop shafts and he was called one evening at 6pm and told to go to Fodens in Darlington, collect a new prop shaft and proceed to Cannock. He arrived just after midnight, helped the fitter to fix on the new shaft and got back home at a 5.45am. Fully expecting at least part of the day off, he was somewhat taken aback when he was told, that breakdown job was yesterday, today is another day and to get back to work. Whenever he was acting as 'mate' he admits to taking some stick from the men. He was often given the dirtiest jobs to do and when it came to settling down in some

The make up of the Sunter's Board of Directors after the take over.

dodgy digs while on a long run, he would be told to 'take that bed over there as it's the best one in the room'. Almost invariably it was the coldest dampest bed in the room, but he took it all on the chin and the men accepted him for it. So Peter Sunter the heir to the company was dropped in at the bottom end and left to get on with it. His father had warned him that he would have to prove to all in the company that he had not been born with a silver spoon in his mouth. Peter learned very quickly how true that was.

With driving Tom Sunter to various meetings and receptions, Peter gained a valuable insight into the procedures and met many of top people in the industry as Tom always insisted that he join him at those events. This was obviously another one of Tom Sunter's forward thoughts. This experience was to stand Peter in good stead for the future and in his own words, 'I grew up very quickly'. Although Tom Sunter was known to be a hard taskmaster, he always said thank you whenever Peter carried out a particular task. By contrast, he never once heard his father say thank you that's a job well done. Len Sunter would tell other people that Peter was doing very well and he was pleased with him, but did not say it to Peter.

There was one other member of the family who acted as chauffer to Tom Sunter and that was his daughter Ann who came of driving age in 1962 but had not yet passed her test. Ann chauffeured her father from his home, to Northallerton, and local runs in the Rolls Royce with 'L' plates on back and front, the sight of which in all probability turned a few heads.

Tom's range of travel became more limited due to his visual impairment causing his perception of light to be drastically reduced, and this was having a knock on effect in his business dealings. His nephew Malcolm with his contacts in the world of medicine knew of an eye surgeon in Oxford by the name of Victor Purvis whom he thought might be able to improve Tom's sight surgically. It was a precarious gamble but the impairment was such that it was a chance worth taking. Tom went into hospital but sadly the worst occurred. Tom Sunter died from a heart attack shortly after coming out of the operating theatre. Thus ended the life of a remarkable businessman, respected employer and Man o' the Dales. He was laid to rest in the Church cemetery in Gunnerside along side other family members.

Needless to record, Tom Sunter's death produced devastation in the family business of which he had been pivotal. Owing to his foresight and inner feelings he had tentatively made provision for such an eventuality, which perhaps underlined the measure of his instincts for forward planning. Some time after the death of Tom Sunter, the family had a meeting with Campbell Wardlaw the company solicitor to decide what to do with the business, i.e. to put it up for sale. There were two interested parties, F.R.Evans of Leeds and United Transport. One of their competitors in the heavy haulage business was Wynn's and Percy Wynn, the Managing Director had taken steps to sell his business to United Transport. Peter stated that the best option would to be to sell to the same company. Peter who attended the meeting and the discussions about the proposed sale, suggested that as a safeguard, the land on Boroughbridge Road where the depot was sited should be held and not become part of any proposed sale, this way, there was always a possibility of a way back. His suggestion was dismissed on the grounds that he was too young and inexperienced to know. In the end the decision was made to sell to United Transport.

In 1964, a Labour Government seemed a distinct possibility and with the experiences of the government after the war and all that state control meant, they decided to sell. So the deal was struck and Sunter Brothers joined Robert Wynn's at United Transport. There was one concession and both companies were allowed to keep their individual names and colour schemes, which was good business practice. So to all intents and purposes nothing had changed from the point of view of the works force and indeed for the people of Northallerton. Anyone applying for a job still would apply to Sunters. The formation of the new board of directors for the company was:

As the takeover was completed so were the salaries that Len Sunter and his son Peter were to receive and an extremely bizarre arrangement it was. The company allotted £5,000 per annum to be shared between the two of them. In the first year Len was to receive £3,500 and Peter £1,500. The following year, Len's salary was reduced to £3,000 and Peter's increased to £2,000, This went on for three more years and by the end of the five year period, Len was earning£1,500 and Peter £3,500. In that period, their respective salaries had been reversed without so much as an extra penny being paid by United Transport. Incredible as it may seem, that was the deal negotiated and accepted. To this day Peter is still at a loss of how such a thing could have been negotiated without so much as a murmur of protest.

Although Peter was only twenty two years of age at the time of the take over, he had sufficient nous to realise very early on that Sunters were being used as a sort of dumping ground for unwanted and rather tired equipment from either the Manchester or Newport depots. Such a move was impeding the planned growth of the company and it was to be some years before the opportunity arose to turn the tables. In 1964 the annual profit made by Sunter Brothers stood at approximately £28,000, a reasonable amount under the competitive circumstances of the day and the relative size of the company. Peter was determined that the company's profitability would increase provided that he was given full backing by United Transport and overcome the influence of Robert Wynn.

Without doubt the long and wide loads that were being delivered by Sunters caused a great deal of disruption and aggravation to the public in general, but that aggravation was felt most by motorists in particular which in turn brought extra problems for police forces everywhere. There follows a transcript of a letter written in August 1963 to Head Wrightson by a frustrated motorist who was also a travelling salesman. Sunters and Head Wrightson co-operated in many long and awkward moves and this particular incident concerned a load travelling near Thirsk. The motorist in question, a Mr. Simpson of Leeds, although clearly angered by being held up for so long behind a slow moving ballasted tractor and trailer, he was also blessed with a puckish sense of humour.

This is a transcript of the letter he fired off to the management of Head Wrightson.

13, Victoria Crescent,
Horsforth.
Leeds.
1.8.63.

Messrs. Head Wrightson & Co. Ltd.

Dear Sirs,
I had the misfortune to be travelling yesterday afternoon on the Thirsk-Boroughbridge road. This, as you may know, is one of those Chestertonian rolling English/drunkard roads. I came up outside Thirsk, on a large lump of metal travelling on a juggernaut, driven by a Mr. Sunter. For mile after mile I travelled at snail pace in company with many more vehicles. A moment came at last to pass this monster, and there emblazoned on its side in fluorescent paint were the words- 'Another load from Head Wrightson'.
I have no doubt you are all proud of your efforts in fabricating this super, colossal, gigantic whateveritis. No doubt you broke a bottle of vintage Vaux over it, and I suppose your PRO boys could tell you that your board of directors could be hidden inside and still leave room for half of the boardroom table; or that if you stuck brown paper over the end, you could stuff ten million ping pong balls into it. It might even accommodate half the fuming motorists creeping on behind plus the contents of their overheated radiators.
All of which leaves me cold.
       As a commercial traveller, I had an appointment in Boroughbridge but when I reached there, my customer had given me up and gone home.
May I make a suggestion:
Could you not arrange with your friend Sunter, to have the whole contraption floodlit and travel by night? During the day he could hide away in some secluded lay-by out of harms way, and pass the daylight hours, sleeping, eating and playing patience. I make this suggestion without the expectation of payment.
       It is unfortunate that you are sweating away making these gadgets in the reign of the second Elizabeth. Can you imagine what would have happened if Good Queen Bess had caught up with you on her way to York. You would have been arraigned for obstructing the Queen's highway and preventing free passage of her subjects on their lawful occasions. She would have had your 'head right off son' (sorry about that) and Master Sunter would have dangled from the gibbet in Thirsk, for aiding and abetting. Fortunately for you, you are able to travel on the Marples highway and that garrulous man would have passed you by on the inside on his bike without a word.
Some weeks ago I was held up for miles by a ships propeller, (fortunately the ship was not attached) but there was not a word to tell us who made it.
May I suggest that the next time you send one of these monsters on its way, you attach a luggage label, just in case it gets mislaid. Had you done so on the present occasion you would not have received this letter.
                                                        Yours   sincerely.   G.B.   Simpson.

The Two Diamond 'T's

YPT85 Passing through
Kirkgate, Thirsk

TUP5 heading up with a
Constructor
and the Rotinoff

Diamond T TUP5
in the livery
and name of
Crook and Willington Carriers

Passing through Middlesbrough

The inevitable roundabout
at South Parade, Northallerton

Bob Fletcher with Police outrider pulling out of a depot in his Volvo. c 1974

Les Taylor leaning against the old faithful AEC LPY 256. c 1954

John Robinson in Super Constructor KVN 860E leaving Head Wrightsons, bound for ICI while Ivan Costick strides alongside. c 1968

Although loads like the one depicted, in the letter caused disruption to the likes of Mr. Simpson, they were the lifeblood of the company, but for some time there had been a discernable slow down in the work being allocated to them by the parent company, United Transport. HP Wynn was wont to show Peter the orders he had won from international industries such as Ferranti, A.E.I and Hawker Siddely etc, but very little of this work came the way of Sunters. However there was a bonus for the men in the yard at Northallerton when in May 1964 the company merged with Bulwark United Transport itself a member of British Electric Traction Group. Bulwark ran a fleet of lager tankers and as they were all from the same Group they were entitled to call at any depot for fuel. Whenever a Bulwark tanker made a call at Sunters depot, the men in the yard would grab their prepared containers, i.e. freshly scrubbed hand cleansing buckets, go to the back of the tanker and pour themselves several gallons of lager and have a liquid refreshment break. It must be remembered

KVN 860E Carrying a French Poclain Shovel passing through an unnamed village enroute to Sheffield. John Easton is the 'Wire Man' Bill Jemison the driver and Peter Christon the mate climbing aboard.

that each bucket had a capacity of five gallons! They soon discovered that pouring it out at such a rate made the beer froth thus reducing the quantity of ale. They soon remedied this by 'inventing' a hose connector for the outlet pipe of the tanker that gave them their 'fair share' of proper lager. Len Sunter heard of the stunt and joined his men for a drink. Peter Sunter strove to put a stop to the drinking, but one suspects he wasn't entirely successful in his quest.

Peter and his father were well aware of the fall in orders and work and in Peter's own words he said 'we had to make a move' and this they did. To further this aim they purchased fourteen x 3.65 meters wide axles from Nicolas of France that would match up with Wynn's trailers, thus allowing them to take on some of the work allotted to that company. They did receive a quota of work but in reality the trailers were truly not ideal for the tasks given. They weren't simply trailers to be hooked up and towed away, but had to be configured to various lengths and widths, which took a lot of manpower and time, and in consequence they were expensive to operate. For extremely large loads, a trailer had to be configured to one and half widths. If the load did not fill the specified width, the full size still had to be paid for, causing customers to ask questions. Not only were the trailers labour intensive to build they had to have steering end beams which were very expensive to buy. Taking them on low loaders was tried but, in Peter's words, travelling to Wallsend at 19 feet wide was something of a nightmare.

There was a specialist Nicolas crew organised for the configuring of the trailers, they were, Peter Broughton, David Taylor, Philip Braithwaite (Jr) and Jamie Fraser. When the Nicolas trailers became the norm, those four men would travel everywhere to set them up for the loading tasks. They would have to give Head Office an estimate as to how long it might take to get to the loading point the time required to have the trailers made ready. Almost always they added on an extra day to their calculations so that they could have a day off sight and pub seeing.

In the midst of all this ordering and change Peter married Christine Forth at the All Saints Church in Northallerton on the 5th of June 1965. A honeymoon was a welcome break from the rigours and pitfalls of the business, but all too soon it was back to the yard and back organising the company.

Just as things started to pick up, Peter's father took his retirement and left Peter as the manager of the entire business in Northallerton. Peter was now on his own and it was he who had to carry the can for Sunters. So in 1966 at the tender age of 24, the task fell to him to build up the business and drag it out of the stultifying effects of the merger. One of the first vehicle purchases Peter made on becoming the manager was for the 6x6 Scammel Super Constructor KVN680E. This tractor was to give sterling service for many years.

Len - Sybil - Christine and Peter Sunter

Peter and Christine on their wedding day
5th June 1965

Sunter

Brothers

In Colour

The Rotinoff Atlantic, newly painted prior to departing for the Science Museum of Transport in 1981

The Atkinson Omega

Super Constructor 447 DPY driven by John Robinson (hiding) on the way to Loch Leven, secretly photographed by Ted Stokes while John Wright and Brian Brown look on.

The same
Scammel in the
livery of
Topcliffe Garage.
447 DPY is now
owned by David
Weedon of York
and is being
repainted in the
maroon and grey
of Sunters

Romanby Road into Northallerton
High Street blocked by a large load,

. . . almost clear

David Murphy and his Bride Lesley on their wedding day 16th September 1972

The Super Constructor 'wedding car'

Axles

Two examples of axles configuration.

*A sequence of a
typical Sunter/ITM loadout.
Using a variety of
ballasted tractors.*

Load Variations

The Mallard on the way to
Stewart's Lane
before leaving for York

A super constructor taking
The Mallard out of
Clapham Rail museum

No load was ever refused?

A Scania with a light
but awkward load.

One of the Stothart & Pitt cranes being
moved from Alexander Dock Hull.

Shipping Orders

Ken Bickerton in his Merc. Titan unlaoding a module from the Aberthaw Fisher

Sunters and Wynns working as a team

Two of the many types of seagoing vessels utilised by Sunters for loadouts.

Stan Sygmuta in Scania 142/420 outside British Aerospace with a load bound for Southern Italy in 1985. The slogan on the front is Paso-Pou-Qui' 'He passed this way'. Stan is wearing his desert wellies (sandals)

Terry Thompson on a wintery Lincolnshire Road

Peter Clarke passing through Piccadilly, with a London tram in tow.

A Record Breaker

The Tractomas, nitric acid column and Albert Lowes

*A nitric acid column measuring 221ft x 17ft wide and weighing 285 tons
carried on a Nicolas trailer with 184 wheels and 18 axles travelling
through Billingham to ICI on the 25th March 1984. The lead tractor is the Tractomas,
driven by Albert Lowes and the rear tractor is the Mercedes Titan driven by Malcom Johnson.
In reserve was a second Titan driven by Alan Massie.*

Albert Lowes with Paul Campbell who is wearing his Jim'll Fix it medallion.

One of the many Sunter models now on sale. The Diamond 'T' TUP 5 is featured.

The Sunter Girls & Malcolm White

Margaret Sunter
(Tom Sunter)

Audrey Sunter
(Joseph Sunter)

Margaret Sunter - Mallie - Ann - Malcolm White

Margaret Sunter,
daughter of Joeseph
and Audrey

Peter and Christine Sunter's Daughters
Nicola - Tracy - Clare

Dorothy and Olga,
Len and Sybil Sunter's two daughters.

Peter Sunter - Manager

Once Peter had got used to the idea that he was the one to carry the can, the future brightened and such over used sayings about 'clouds and silver linings and 'doors closing and opening' seemed very apt. The acquisition of those trailers coincided with the boom in the North Sea oil exploration and expansion of the Off and On shore oil industries. This was an opportunity that Peter was not going to let pass, and went for the business with as much drive as he could muster. In the meantime Sunter Brothers carried on as they had always done, that is they delivered long and awkward loads nation wide with a variety of axles and trailers. A new addition to their heavy fleet, the crew cabbed 6 x 4 Scammel Super Contractor TPY860H made its entry at Boroughbridge Road, which in terms of comfort, speed and pulling power was sensational. Sunters were a little tardy in bringing in this model as their rivals Pickfords and Wynns had been using them for some time. Over reliance on the Contractors had not been best for the company.

By the mid 1970s, the faithful Rotinoff Atlantic had also come to the end of its useful working life. Not wanting to see it sold off and being cut up in a nondescript scrap yard, the Science Museum was contacted and asked if they would be interested in accepting it for their Museum of Transport, with the proviso that it was to be on permanent loan. The offer was readily accepted and the Rotinoff was dispatched to Ted Hannan's garage at Etherly in County Durham and given a sound mechanical servicing and the paintwork was stripped down and a fresh coating of the red and grey livery was applied. The proud logo of 'Sunter Brothers of Northallerton' was emblazoned above the cab and on the doors and eleven months later she was ready to go. It was in 1975 when the 'Rot' was retired that John Robinson its chauffeur since its arrival at the yard also took his leave from driving and delivering heavy loads. He was given a car a map a pen and promoted to Routes Officer. Not only was it a good thing for John to get off the 'heavy' road, it made good sense to have his experience of roads and routes put to good use.

By this time Peter had been making regular trips to the continent visiting other heavy haulage companies and taking notes. He noticed that operators there were using 3 metre wide modular trailers as opposed to the 3.65 metre size used by Sunters. One immediate advantage was that they could be configured in half a day instead of the three days it took at the present, a huge saving both in manpower and costs. Peter thought hard and long about this but was convinced that these were what were needed at Boroughbridge Road, but he also did some sideways thinking. Realising that if he made contact with HP Wynn about the possible purchase, he would get a big no-no. He then realised that if he went to the French owned Nicolas Trailer Company, they would immediately get onto HP Wynn and that would once again stop the move. Peter decided to pay a visit to Scheueler in Germany. He put the plan for trailers with a capacity of 1,000 tonnes to Dieter Krah; Scheueler's Trailer's export manager and waited for his response. Dieter replied with the message "you have a very good idea but you will never get away with this package, as soon as United Transport find out, they will tell you to go-Nicolas, but I will make up the package and await further correspondence". At the next Board meeting HP Wynn asked, " Peter what are you going to surprise us with tomorrow?" Peter replied, "I don't want to spoil your meal tonight, so I'll wait until tomorrow" and that is what he did. They met the next day and Peter presented his plans, stressing that the modular trailers could be built to 10 x 100 ton or 1 x 1000 tonnes configuration. HP was very cold about the idea, and Duncan Folds the Chairman asked "What orders have you got for these new trailers?" Peter's reply was starkly honest. "In sequence, none and I don't know, but without it we will not get any at all, I cannot go seeking orders and then be asked if I have the wherewithal to do the job, I need to be able to say we have the equipment and the expertise to do the task" The board were not moved in the first instance, but after a month of explanations and research, they were convinced and agreed for Peter to go ahead and purchase the trailers.

Work for those trailers came their way and so Peter's gamble had paid off. They worked with an American Company based at Tees-side by the name of Rigging International and became their 'trailer arm' to quote Peter's phrase. The work with Rigging International lasted for some while, but then there was another turn in the fortunes of the company. Three men who were employed by Rigging International decided to leave and set up in business on their own. The three were, Alf Duffield, Brian Pearson and John Wilson and together they formed ITM (International Transport Management). They asked Peter if he would be willing to work with them. Peter said that he could not withdraw from his commitments to Rigging International just like that, and he reminded them that they had to establish themselves in the market, but he would not close the door on them.

Having set up a Continental Division under the management of Roger Hobson, there was the occasional trip to the Continent searching for business. On one such trip Peter came across a new design of trailer, a 6 axle semi low loader on hydraulic suspension. Some months later a modified version in Sunter's livery was being exhibited by the manufacture Goldhofer Fahrzeugwerk GmbH & Co at the Frankfurt Commercial Vehicle Show. All previous trailers had been fitted with a rigid neck, which was totally unsuitable for Sunter operations. In collaboration with Goldhofer's engineers, a hydraulic neck was fitted to the Sunter trailer. In the past, the company had encountered problems with refractory lined heater modules and if they were not offloaded with extreme care, the concrete lining would crack. The new Goldhofer trailer with the hydraulics and rigid neck for transporting the lighter modules was a great advance.

Peter was then invited by Goldhofer to spend the opening day of the show on their stand and so he decided to call on Rigging International at their Wimbledon HQ to discuss their future requirements in view of recent developments. After confirming that Sunters would honour all outstanding contracts and all future ones, Rigging International in turn confirmed that they would deal only with Sunters in view of the good service and excellent co-operation they had enjoyed over the recent years. That same evening Peter joined the Managing Director of Goldhofer for dinner. During the evening the MD asked 'Who are Rigging International?' Peter explained who they were and gave the details of the relationship enjoyed by them and Sunters. The MD then informed Peter that they, Rigging had just ordered 40 hydraulic axle lines which equated to 1,000 tons capacity. To say that Peter was somewhat taken aback would be an understatement but he had been in the business long enough to know that realism is what is needed and there was nothing for him to do but to accept that such dirty tricks were part and parcel of the competition in the heavy haulage industry, and so he decided to contact ITM. Within a very short time of him finding out about the shock trailer deal by Rigging, there was a press announcement, 'Pickfords-ITM' joint partnership'. The three men who had formed ITM had joined up with Pickfords to do their work. This second set back was not quite so bad as it first appeared. Management is not just about securing contracts etc, it is also about knowing the strengths and weaknesses of competitors, and Peter knew the weaknesses of Pickfords. He had known for some time that they had the same trailer set up, viz 3.65 metre widths, as Wynns and he knew that they would struggle to meet time schedules and costs. His instincts were correct. After Pickfords had done a couple of loadouts for ITM, Alf Duffield contacted Peter and asked if he could help. Alf told Peter that he must offer the next load to Pickfords but they did not have sufficient trailers for the module loadout and they would have to subcontract a 21 axle trailer plus a tractor and crew from Sunters. The contract was for the loadout of two modules at the Leith facility of the Motherwell Bridge Offshore. This was an opportunity not to be missed, with Pickfords having only 3.65m wide equipment; it was known at Sunters that it would take them forever to mobilise. Peter called in Charles Tompkins the company engineer and explained the situation. After a short discussion between the two, it was decided to completely mobilise the trailer in Northallerton yard and fully test the steering and integral hydraulics. A 21 axle trailer had not been configured before and by undertaking a test run; any problems would be overcome in Northallerton rather than at Leith. On completion of the test, the trailer was split into a 13 axle and an 8 axle. The steering arrangement was adjusted on the 13 axle trailer for the road journey to Leith whilst the 8 axle remained as per test and carried on top of the 13 axle. Everyone in Northallerton realised the importance of the contract and the far reaching effects it could have on the future development of the company, so orders were given that under no circumstances was anyone on site to be told of the trial assembly. The 'road show' arrived on site on the Friday evening with a view to commencing the site assembly at 8.pm on the Saturday morning. There was a slight delay as the crane driver had slept in and the 8 axle was not lifted off until 9.30pm. Notwithstanding the late start, the 21 axle was assembled and tested by 1pm. By comparison, Pickfords, who had arrived on site on the Thursday night and despite working through the night of Sunday, were not completely rigged until Monday afternoon.

ITM then obtained a follow on contract at Burntisland on the north bank of the Firth of Forth and after a site meting it was decided that the quickest and most economical method of mobilising the equipment would be by barge. This method was adopted and the contract was successfully concluded by the following Sunday night. On the following Wednesday, Peter was with Alf Duffield when a call from the

Managing Director of Burntisland saying that Pickfords were still on site and stressed the point that a claim for extra charges would not be entertained as the other trailer had left the site on the Monday morning. Peter was able to reassure the MD that payment would not be asked for. Sometime later two site moves were undertaken at the Charlton Leslie site on the Tyne for ITM, using all Sunter equipment. The plan had worked and it signalled the beginning of the end of the Pickfords-ITM partnership. As a result of all this, Sunters were asked to submit, along with other recognised European contractors, a quotation for the sea and land transportation contract for the reconstruction of the BP Sullom Voe oil terminal. Peter and Alf Duffield attended the pre-tender meeting at London Offices of Constructor John Brown. As they were waiting for their interview, John Wynn appeared out of the meeting room and all voiced surprise at being there without prior knowledge and John Wynn left stating that they were not interested in the contract because shipping was involved.

Owing to problems associated with site accommodation at Sullum Voe, the designers decided to modularise as much of the plant as was possible, so the PAR-Pre-assembled Rack and the PAU-Pre-assembled Unit were born. As all items were to be encased in concrete based fire proofing, a very strict deflection criterion was specified in the tender document with particular attention being paid to trailer movements. Charles Tompkins and Nicolas (Trailers) took care of the trailer deflection analysis bearing in mind the many different configurations that would be used. Being a marine orientated company, ITM looked closely at the various shipping methods available. It soon became obvious that the type of vessel the client anticipated using, could not be, due to the deflection criterion stipulated. No one had thought about the consequences of deflection during marine movements, only ITM. As a consequence Sunters/ITM won the contract that involved collecting and delivering, on several barges, more than 60 items of onshore structures weighing from 70 tons up to 300 tons from Antwerp, Middlesbrough, Wallsend and Leith to Sullum Voe.

The original time scale for the work was approximately two months to be actually spent on site at Sullum Voe, but Sunters were so up front with theirs and ITM's expertise, the job lasted two and half years and made a lot of money for both companies. It was here that the Ro-Ro (roll on roll off-loadout) system of transportation utilising barges was first used. It was another learning curve for all involved. Learn as Sunters did, it did not mean that the job went smoothly, far from it. At that time there was a national lorry drivers strike that was proving to be very effective. The work force at Sunters although union orientated was by no means as militant in the sense of that some big industries were at that time. If there was a member who was inclined to be militant, for instance the formidable John Easton, he was placed on a workers committee and allowed to voice his opinions and ideas, this had the effect of allowing him to see the over-riding difficulties faced by the company and the industry as well as the employees. The lorry driver's strike was all about pay and Peter convened a meeting with his work force and laid it on the line. He told them that the few pence involved was not worth them all losing their jobs which included his job, because that is what would happen if they lost the Sullum Voe contract. The men trusted Peter and his word and decided to carry on and finish the contract. The men who went to Sullum Voe decided amongst themselves to pool all their overtime pay and at the end of the contract share it out amongst the ones who were not directly involved in the work. Whichever way you look at it, that was a very generous gesture.

Not only did Sunters make a lot of money from the Sullum Voe contract, they ended up with more hydraulic axles than any other heavy hauler in Europe and were well over the £1,000,000 in profit, a great deal more than the £28,000 made in 1966 even allowing for the differing values of the pound for the times. An example of

Super Contractor TPY 675H (later YVN 308T) passing through Dunnington near York with the Chinese locomotive destined for the National Rail Museum.

Bob Fletcher leading a carriage of 'The Orient Express'

Peter's acumen was shown when they were asked to tender for a contract to move twelve heat exchangers each weighing 76 tons each to be moved from Glasgow to Tilbury for a German company. The opposition for the contract was Pickfords. Peter calculated that Pickfords would bid £6000 (per load) for the job and decided to bid £5000 per load and needless to say Sunters got the job. Within ten weeks, they had moved all twelve heat exchange units to Tilbury and made £60,000 via a trailer that cost £27,000. These sets of trailers were to make Sunters a lot more money and create a lot of work. It was some time before the other hauliers got the message and followed suit. Peter stresses that the success of the company was as much due to the men in the yard and the staff in the office. He often sought the advice of the crews who were going to do the actual moving as they were the ones with whom ultimate success or failure rested. So in that sense, Sunters in essence were still a family run business despite merging with a larger company.

Contract work moving rig modules on site for the oil industry was becoming the norm for the heavy hauliers, but there was still a considerable amount of heavy road haulage business available. Shortly after the Sullum Voe contract, Sunters-ITM was given the task of carrying the Thames Barrier gates that had been built at the Cleveland Bridge fabrication yard on Tees-side. There were four main gates each weighing 1,500 tonnes and stretched almost 200 feet in length. They were loaded onto the Nicolas hydraulic suspension trailers, safely delivered and loaded onto the moored barges without any real problems. Another high profile job, high profile inasmuch as that it was headline new for many weeks moving of the famed Mary Rose warship. The Mary Rose made the headlines for many months as the hulk that had been lying in deep water for many centuries and was finally brought to the surface with a great deal of difficulty and many anxieties. In the grand scheme of the raising and moving of the Mary Rose, Sunters played an insignificant part.

A further move by Sunters was when they had a chain of agents who specialised in 'abnormal loads' placed in all important European seaports and capitals. Cross Channel and North Sea loadouts were carried out using the Ro-Ro system and undertaken almost daily on what was called door-to-door delivery. The trailer fleet had to conform to EEC standards; that is all must have automatic and manual steering. The work in Europe not only covered what might be called the democratic countries but also the 'Iron Curtain' countries as well. Although difficulties were many in the former Soviet dominated states, working in such countries as Italy and Spain etc could cause plenty of hassle for crews by the local police who liked to be 'taken care of'. In East Germany passing through 'Check-point Charlie' the entry into Berlin was a veritable nightmare as were many of the other border posts. An almost microscopic inspection of the vehicle and its documents was the usual starting point by the border guards. The back handing of currency of the day was considered the norm for a driver to be able to proceed. In the western countries, if money was not the answer, the check point police would take the driver to a restaurant of fairly high quality, order all manner of food items for themselves and blandly pass the bill over to the driver. Long serving driver Les Taylor even had the indignity of being held incommunicado for a while over some supposed infringement of local law.

Drivers became very worldly wise after a few sojourns to the continent.

As loads increased in weight, it was realised that the pulling power of the tractors had to match those weights. As valiant as the Scammel Contractors were performing, they were beginning to show their age and weariness. Peter Sunter, rather than buy another new Contractor, carried out a costing exercise into the possibilities of a rebuild of the oldest model of the fleet. Roy Pickard with Bob Lincoln and Ted Beasley were charged with removing anything that could be removed from the first Contractor purchased by the company and have it sent for a major refit and makeover. It was given a new wood panelled cab made and fitted by Plaxtons of Scarborough and an engine rebuild. Six months later the result was the metamorphosis of Contractor TPY 675H into Contractor YVN 308T. To all intents and purposes it was a brand new ballasted tractor complete with a catwalk around the ballast box and improved power steering, which was greatly appreciated by regular driver Jimmy 'Gino' Goulding.

Peter realised that still more muscle was required and went in search of newer vehicles and in the mid summer of 1978 he decided to strengthen the fleet with the purchase of another 6x4 tractor this also being a 'foreign import' The Mercedes Titan Reg. No. VVN 910S that arrived at the depot was a left hand drive and in many respects a hybrid of a vehicle. It sported the Merc three pointed star and cab, and had a huge Mercedes 21 litre engine, but it was built by Titan of Appenweier and set

A spectacular night off loading operation.

98

A pair of Super Contractors in a rare side pushing operation. Note the angle of the axles.

Sunters back a cool £63,000. The Titan was purchased as a dual purpose vehicle in that it could be utilised as either an artic or a ballasted tractor. Unlike the Contractors that had semi automatic fluid flywheel gearboxes, the Titan had an eight speed synchromesh gearbox with a special crawler gear. The arrival of this vehicle added pulling power to Sunter's heavy stable of tractors, but within a few weeks of it going into service, it developed a few problems and lost that power. Ken Bickerton who was the regular driver of the Titan reported a dramatic loss of power and a constant vibration when ever the vehicle was under load. The Titan was returned to the manufactures where it was discovered that the prop shaft was set at the wrong angle. The problem was soon sorted out and the Titan was back on the road vibration free, but still with its apparent loss of power.

In the late 1970s the Sunter fleet of heavies stood at:

Ballasted Tractors

HVN 397N		197	Scammell	Contractor	6x4	240	tonnes	GTW
LAJ 398P	S	198	Scammell	Contractor	6x4	240	tonnes	GTW
NAJ 103P		303	Scammell	Contractor	6x4	240	tonnes	GTW
YVN 308T (TPY 675H)		308	Scammell	Contractor	6x4	240	tonnes	GTW
CVN 483L	S	183	Scania	140	6x4	120	tonnes	GTW
HVN 396N	S	196	Volvo	F89	6x4	120	tonnes	GTW

Artic Units 4x2

DAJ 584L		184	Scania 110
PAJ 989M	S	189	Volvo F89
PVN 590M	S	190	Scania 110
PVN 691M	S	191	Scania 110
GVN 893N	S	193	Scania 110
JAJ 794N		194	Scania 110
NAJ 99P	S	199	Volvo F89
OVN 675R	S	304	Scania 111
OVN 684R	S	305	Scania 111

Heavy Artic Units 6x4

BPY 82L	S	182	Scania 110
DPY 185L		183	Scania 110 with lift up axle
OAJ 288M		188	Scania 110
PVN 692M	S	192	Volvo 140
GVN 995R	S	195	Volvo F89
NAJ 101P	S	301	Volvo F89
NAJ 102P	S	302	Volvo F89
OVN 676R	S	306	Volvo
VVN 910S	S	307	Mercedes 'Titan' 26.32
YPY 209T	S	309	Scania 141

S Denotes Sleeper Cab.

The Rotinoff Atlantic was still held at the depot but no longer operational There was also a mixed bag of 3 tonners, pick-ups and vans. Also Len Sunter had purchased two steamrollers that were parked at the furthest end of the depot. They were used on occasion for rolling rubble and aggregate when ever the yard had to be extended.

Still the pulling power of the company increased. Within a year the mighty 6x6 Renault cabbed Tractomas powered by a Cummins engine and built by trailer makers Nicolas of France, joined the mighty Titans at Sunters. The 'Handbook' on the Tractomas supplied by the manufacturer states that the vehicle could cope with 250 tons, Sunters found that although it could cope with five times that weight with ease, it did have a tendency to throw second gears. The Tractomas was to become the charge of Albert Lowes another stalwart of the company. Eighteen months later, a second Titan was purchased, EJW 229V and this became the charge of Malcolm Johnson. This Titan was very similar to the previous one but had a 6x6 capability and was first and foremost a ballasted tractor. The twin Titans proved their pulling power

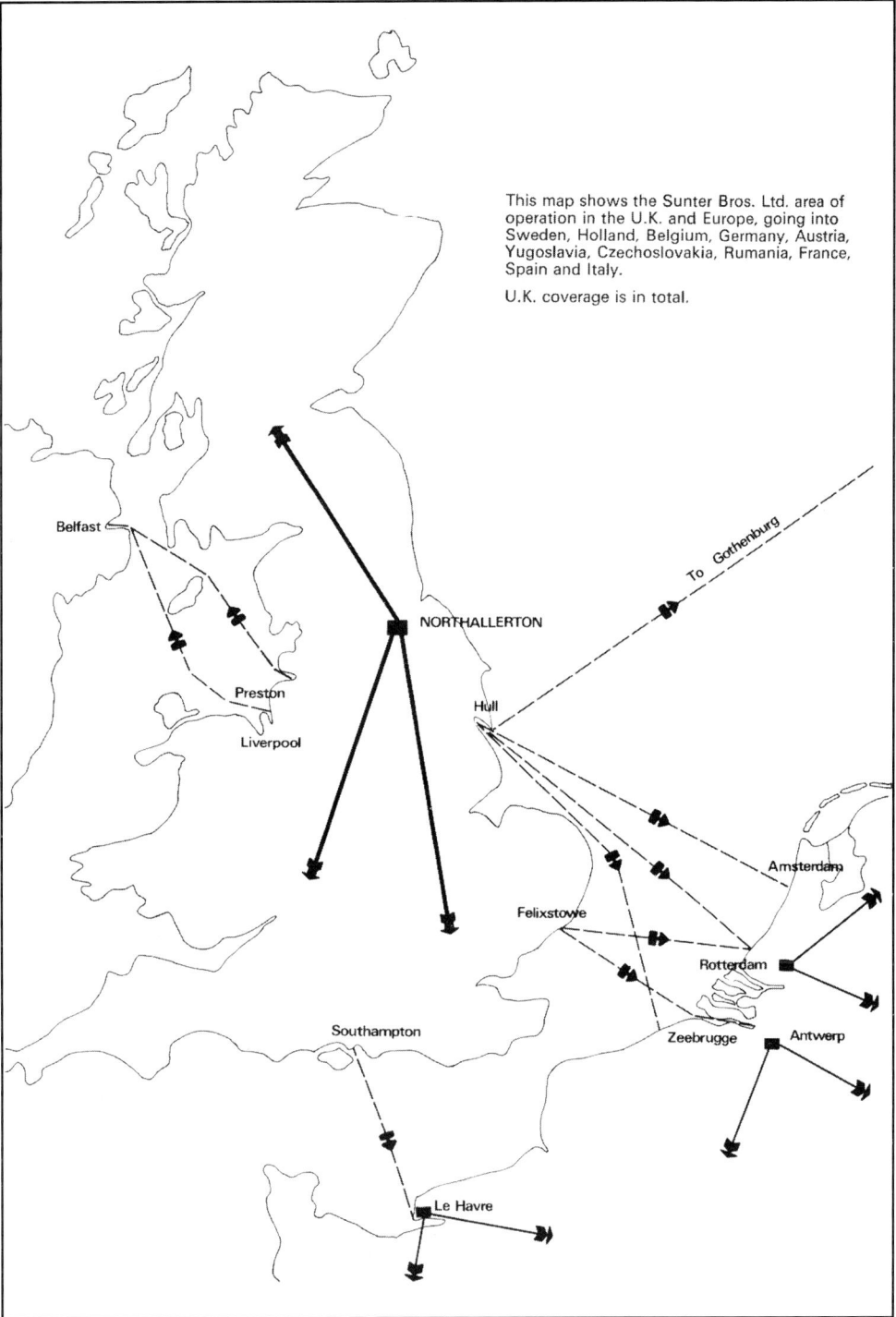

This map shows the Sunter Bros. Ltd. area of operation in the U.K. and Europe, going into Sweden, Holland, Belgium, Germany, Austria, Yugoslavia, Czechoslovakia, Rumania, France, Spain and Italy.

U.K. coverage is in total.

A map showing the extent of Sunter Brothers operarations in Europe.

and the two drivers proved their driving skills when they hauled a production module bound for the Fulmar oil field across the site on 98 axles carried on 800 tyres. The module weighed in at a spectacular 2,400 tonnes

In June1981 the faithful Rotinoff was ready to go. A set of trailers, axles and wheels were all part of the deal for her transportation by low loader to the former RAF airfield of Wroughton near Swindon. Bob Fletcher a Volvo artic driver had the honour of taking that stalwart of many outsize loads to its final resting place. So now that special Rotinoff Atlantic GR7 holds pride of place in the museum among many other exhibits. It was special insomuch as it was one of only two that truly operated as a heavy tractor on Britain's highways. The Swiss Army went on to buy several Rotinoffs and two ended up in Australia, but sadly as good as the vehicle was, the model never really made it in large numbers in the world of heavy haulage. With the death of George Rotinoff, Atkinsons took over the company and built a model called the Atkinson Omega, which was similar to the original, but it never really made the grade. Sunters purchased an Omega Reg. MPY 63F that had a Cummings 250bhp engine and an Allison automatic gearbox. The Omega worked for several years with the company and at a distance the untrained eye could mistake it for a Rotinoff. In 1989 the Sunter Rotinoff made one last foray on the road. Roy Pickard was invited to by the Science Museum curator to take it on the London to Brighton vintage commercial vehicle run. It was transported from Wroughton to London by low loader and driven to Brighton, completing the run in a creditable 3 hours. It was then taken back to the museum on the low loader. A memorable swan song for a fine vehicle.

While Peter had been organising the relocation of the Rotinoff, his father, Len Sunter co-founder of the company died. Len had worked for and with the company since 1930 and a lot of the credit for its success was down to this straightforward yet at times complicated man. Guile and finesse were never his forte, but down to earth straight to the point actions were. On the day of his burial, almost all of the employees of the company attended his funeral. It so happened that David Murphy was due to be married on that very same day, and the throng of guests shared out their time between the wedding and funeral. Len Sunter was laid to rest in the Gunnerside church cemetery along side the other members of his family and was sadly missed by his family, the community and by all who knew and worked with him.

The Persian Gulf was the next phase in the Sunter-ITM saga. Considerable work was being created in that part of the Middle East. Peter was called to Saudi Arabia to supervise the moving of engines each weighing 175 tons at £750,000 per engines over 280 rough and ready miles. Two Autocars of Odeh Naber Transport with Goldhoffer trailers with twelve axles were utilised and it was Sunters expertise that was on hire, not their equipment. Work had to be provided for the local workers and the local economy. The route taken from Aqaba in Jordan to Tabouk Power Station in Saudi Arabia. climbed 7,500ft in nine miles, creating great strain on the towing vehicles. The route was littered with discarded and shattered engine parts of previous 'desert trains', testimony to the rugged and dangerous terrain. All of this only took place after Peter had travelled out to photograph and measure the road network so as to ascertain the weight loading of all the bridges en-route. As it turned out, many of the bridges were hardly built to take the loads, but they did?? The final installation being undertaken by the Black Gang.

Another contract was secured and this meant a wholesale move to Dubai for the team for the work to begin. But before they began there was a change in the usual Sunter livery. The distinctive maroon and grey colour scheme of their fleet was changed to a dominating white albeit with a red bar down the centre of the ballast boxes of the tractors. The name was changed from Sunter/ITM to The Hercules International Transport Co. Ltd. The task was to move by barge, six huge spherical balls or to give them their proper name, pressure surge spheres from the CMP fabrication yard at Aman to Zirku Island and haul them two miles to their destination. Each sphere weighed in at 200 tonnes and had a diameter of 53ft. Sunter/ITM Nicolas trailers with its hydraulic suspension and its in-built jacking system guaranteed stable on and off loading. Needless to say everything went to plan.

On completion of those Middle East contracts, Peter Sunter had been attending board meetings almost weekly. These interruptions as he saw them interfered with his running of the depot in Northallerton. When he said as much, the other directors told him that he was too close to the work-force and that he did not have a 'helicopter' view of the situation. Hearing that quaint 'avant garde' expression has remained with Peter and he still smiles at it even today. Through all these meetings and agendas, Peter perceived a subtle but definite change emerging concerning the heavy haulage industry. The whole business and Sunters in particular was being transformed from a heavy road haulage company to a transport engineering company and he knew things had to change for them to survive. He mentioned to the other board members about his observations but was offered virtually no support. He was then moved from Northallerton to Stafford where a purpose built depot had been set up at great expense With great reluctance he moved with his wife and three children down to Stafford into a house that was very much smaller than the one he had left in Northallerton which made for a bad start in his new location.

For Peter, working and living in the Midlands was the nadir of his life in the industry. Some months after his appointment at Stafford he was made the chairman of the Group that is Wynns, Wrekin Roadways and Sunters, which strengthened his arm considerably. Peter worked steadily if somewhat unhappily at Stafford for a number of years and he says, without the support of his wife Christine who was 'a rock' during the difficult times, he is convinced that he would have quit and gone into another business. While at Stafford he played a vital part along with Roger Harries in reorganising a major transport contract that had gone disastrously wrong in the Sudan, but as this is not directly Sunter orientated, this aspect of his life is for another time.

When Peter eventually became Chairman of the Heavy Haulage Group, which now

Dubai
A Super Contractor in the white livery of
Hercules International Transport.

A group of Sunter lads in Dubai.

Two of the pressure spheres at Zirku Island

included Wrekin Roadways, he was authorised to purchase a car up the value of £15,000. After many negotiations with a local BMW dealer, an order was placed for a 728i model. Following his next visit to Chepstow he was told by his immediate boss that he could not have that particular model as it was the same shape as his and people might think they were of the same status. To say that Peter was non-plussed is an understatement. By this time he was beginning to feel uneasy, the major problems in the Sudan had been overcome with absolutely no support from HQ, because no one understood the ins and outs of heavy haulage. A new depot had been designed and built at Stafford without a single visit from a senior executive, a corporate plan had been put forward to change the direction of the company, from a road transport contractor to a transport engineering company with the possible change of alliance within the Group from Tanker Division to Heavy Crane Division. This was turned down and from that time the writing was on the wall despite warnings that if adjustments weren't made the company would suffer and 'major surgery' would be required. Peter was not prepared to have the title of Chairman while not being able to direct the Group in the way he and his colleagues thought best. Heavy Haulage is a very specialised business it cannot be run by committee and this is where Peter felt he was out on a limb with the rest of the executives. Probably the best example of this was after he had resigned, he was offered a seat on the board of a bus company based in Nairobi as an incentive to stay. During the two weeks following his resignation several meetings were convened to persuade him to change his mind. His mind however was made up. There was no turning back but the opportunity was taken to remind all concerned that the proposals he had put forward were the only way forward. If new policies were not invoked, four years on we would all witness the demise of the haulage Group in one form or another, climbing to the top again would be very much harder. There was no satisfaction for Peter in seeing those words come true.

Before we reach the final chapters of the Sunter Story, let us remember some of the funny times, times that were down right ridiculous and sad occurrences that permeated the life of working for Sunters as seen through the eyes and memories of those who witnessed those events. This change of direction was not easy for Peter and even after he left he strove whenever possible to help his Northallerton colleagues to keep them going forward and he kept up his friendship to the end.

Tales from the ...
Highway

Although Heavy Haulage is by definition about tractor and trailer units carrying outsized loads to all corners of the country, a history of any haulage company would not be complete without mention of the myriad of disparate characters within that story. Characters and their escapades of 'The Sunter Story' are legion and some of the funny and not so funny tales must be recorded to give a taste of life with a high profile heavy haulage company. However only a selection of the scores of stories can be related for two reasons, the first is due to space or the lack of it, and the other is to protect families and friends from possible embarrassment and ridicule. Suffice to say there are dark mutterings of an increase in the country's population during the Sunter years?

Hauling shipments of almost any type of material, shape and size on the Queen's highway is without doubt a very skilful and difficult job and occasionally a hazardous one. To the bystander and layman, it appears all that is required is for the driver to climb into his cab, drive away and deliver. The reality is that there are hours of organising, back breaking trailer configurations and loading to say nothing of the long days on the road inching round corners and negotiating over and under what appear to be miniscule bridges. Until the building of the motorway network in the UK, all loads large or small had to be routed through large cities, towns, rural villages and back roads for them to reach their destinations. This was because many routes that had to be taken were never simply straight in or straight out. A relatively short distance may have to have been travelled on a normal route, but with low bridges and tight corners to be negotiated, a tortuous circuit would have to be undertaken. Many a time the driver and mate could see their destination, but would have to a several miles round about route to get to it, thus adding many hours to their journey. Another factor with driving in those early days was that there were no such things as flashing indicators or flashing and occulting lights. The normal method was for the driver to use hand of arm signals, but with wide and awkward loads this was impossible. A mate was an absolute necessity to help with traffic problems and this was usually done by him running along the blind side of the load. When Sunter Brothers began their operations way back in the 1920s, major trunk roads were almost non-existent, but of course so was road traffic. However, road traffic grew faster than expected and with an intervening war, road building went to the bottom of the government's priorities.

This problem of indirect routes was best highlighted by one of the more well known characters to be employed by Sunters, none other than roustabout; Jock Fraser. Jock featured in what must be some sort of a record for distance travelled in relation to time taken and for the load being carried and for trouble caused en route. Jock and Tony Swann, were given a job to collect a drag line excavator from Derby and take it to The China Clay Company quarry at St. Austell in Cornwall, then go on

High - Wide and Awkward

A Nicolas trailer and load shoe-horning' through Ripon City's one way system. The pub sign was saved by an inch.

Another tight squeeze. (Unknown)

It wasn't always the driver's fault. This load had been misdirected by it's police escort going through London. Note the film showing at the Odeon cinema, 'Hell Drivers" the story of heavy goods drivers.

*Two classic examples of a Scammell Constructor negotiating a bridge
and a very tight corner. Location, Hyde Cheshire.*

Where - did you say?
Jock Fraser (centre) studies a route map with Black Gang members,
Des Gibson - ??????? - Bobby Evans - Brian Brown

The ex army AEC converted to the Black Gang's 'Tackle Wagon'.

to collect a smaller excavator from Malvern. The vehicles they took were the Scammel Constructor heading up, and the Foden two stroke pushing plus a ninety-ton trailer. The journey to Derby went according to plan, but the rest was a veritable nightmare. Almost everywhere on the route, Bridgewater, Wells, Yeovil, they met road works, sewers being dug up, closed roads and were re-routed time and again by their police escorts along narrow and patently unsuitable country roads. One route took them through a thin strip of a road called the Rock of Ages. The excavator was fifteen feet wide and on some roads the hedgerows would be stripped of foliage as Jock manoeuvred the front tractor and Tony pushed hard at the rear, the traffic, at the front and rear being snarled up by the score. Eventually they were told to park up and there they stayed for days on end until a road could be cleared for them. In his exasperation, the Chief Constable of the county threatened to have the whole lot cut up and sold as scrap. After two weeks, Tony Swann, had had enough of the problems and phoned the yard at Northallerton telling them he was going home and would return when the load was expected to move, leaving Jock to look after everything. When they finally got back on the move, they entered Launceston in Cornwall where the whole train, tractors and trailer got utterly jammed on a corner due to the narrowness of the road. This not only held up the delivery of the load, already weeks late, it blocked the road in both directions for hours. Tempers flared both police and motorists alike. A lorry load of sleepers to lay under the trailer wheels was ordered from a local firm and the load was painstakingly inched clear. The next problem was a weight-limited bridge. The solution? Take off the trailer and the load, drive the tractors across, attach the winch cable to the trailer and wind it on across the bridge. The winch method was the norm for crossing weight limited bridges. When they finally got going, they were about to enter Redruth when they saw 69 year old Dr. Barbara Moore (famous at that time for her long distance walking) completing the final part of her marathon walk from John O' Groats to Lands End. The excavator was finally delivered to its destination so Jock and Tony set off for the second leg of their journey. They went to Malvern and thence on to Manchester to pick up a Ferranti transformer. The time taken to complete the job was, eight weeks and four days. Jock remarked wryly that Dr. Moore had walked the entire length of Scotland and England in just two weeks!! There were many questions asked by Mr. Tom and Mr. Len when Jock got back, not least about the amount of money that he had 'subbed' while away which totalled some £300. A sum that almost equalled what the job had been costed. Not only was Jock Fraser renowned for that extra long trip, he was famous, or some might say infamous for his personal shenanigans while out on the road. Jock not only impressed his gregarious personality on the company but also gave the mighty Rotinoff what might be called a nom de guerre. Below the sword symbol mounted on the radiator of the Rotinoff, Jock had the word Fearnought proudly emblazoned below. Not only did it seem to symbolise the tractor's personality, it was also the motto of the Royal Tank Regiment. On being asked why he thought of this name, he replied that it was to counter the name Dreadnought that was written on the radiator grill of a Wynn's tractor. Later Fearnought was transferred from the Rotinoff to Scammel Contractor NAJ 103P driven by Peter Clemmett.

Although Jock and Tony took an unprecedented eight weeks for an expected two weeks trip, Jimmy Goulding and Jack Emms must hold the record for the longest time taken to travel the shortest distance. They were to take a load weighing 98 tons from Thornaby to Consett, but as they set off, the winter weather in all its ferocity set in. They encountered snowdrifts that were packed as high as the lead Foden. Jimmy pushing with the Diamond T plugged away, but due to the intense cold, the tow bar suddenly and without warning snapped into two separate pieces. This sent the trailer sliding back into a snowdrift, halting operations at a stroke. Despite the snowdrifts, intense cold, and broken tow bars, they finally arrived at their destination six weeks after setting off from Thornaby, a paltry thirty six miles distant.

While Jock Fraser and Jack Emms along with Peter Clemmett experienced long and tortuous delays with their respective loads, John Robinson and Jock had the opposite problem with one of their loads. In September 1960 they duly left Northallerton with John leading with the Rotinoff and Jock pushing from the rear with the Foden. The load was a 20ft high 180 tons steel section to be delivered to Erith in Kent. They were due to be routed through London but on their arrival at the Metropolitan boundary, their expected police escort had not materialised. After waiting for some considerable time, they contacted the police only to be told in no uncertain terms that they had arrived seven and half days early! It appears that the traffic clerk had misjudged the pulling power of the redoubtable Rotinoff and the expertise of both John and Jock. No way would the Met police try and change the timing for the load and escort to travel through London, so they ordered the load to be pulled in to a lay-by, to be locked up and to be kept there for a week. No way could those two drivers wait that long, so John phoned the Depot at Northallerton and told them the story. Both he and Jock were told to get themselves home pronto.

Bill Jemison, a bluff lad from Durham, was a heavy tractor driver who had previously been employed by Crouche's the dragline excavator specialist of Durham and when he joined Sunters, was entangled in a couple of embarrassing mishaps. Both were with loads while 'piloting' his Scammel Contractor for Sunters. The first was when he was leading a very large, long and expensive cylinder bound for the Soviet Union through the streets of Thornaby-on-Tees, his load being one of three. He was negotiating a roundabout close to the Swan Hotel at the correct speed and position when horrors of horrors, the cylinder fell off the trailer! Chaos reigned for many hours as traffic had to be diverted and heavy-duty cranes brought in to reload the Contractor's trailer. The cause of the load falling off? Bill's steersman,' "who will remain anonymous", was walking as he should have been at the rear of the trailer adjusting the trailer level whenever adverse camber was encountered. This was done by the manipulation of a set of levers which, when activated, raised or lowered the rear of the trailer to compensate. Then it began to rain and the 'steersman' became a little fed up with getting wet and so decided to ride on the rear of the trailer under cover and to operate the levers using his feet. Sitting looking rearwards on the trailer had the effect of transposing his position and transposing his sensory left and right. When the next camber was encountered he pressed the wrong lever and lowered the trailer into the camber instead of raising it. As a result, the trailer sank lower and

Bridges!

Ted Daynes guides Peter Clarke over Morton Bridge Northallerton

The Junior Constructor squeezing under a bridge near Stockton.

'*I approached the accused's lorry, which was stuck under the low bridge, and said in a jocund manner: "Ho ho sir, delivering bridges are we?" . . .*'

I *am indebted to the Editor of the magazine Truck & Driver for permission to publish this very apt cartoon by Shobba* lower causing the cylinder to roll over its chocks and to break it's supporting chains, at which it fell from the trailer. The rest of this chaotic story is shrouded in silence and embarrassment.

On another trip Bill Jemison and his Contractor were collecting an excavator from the city of Lincoln, and they were to witness John Robinson negotiating a long load through the city at the same time. Unfortunately for John, Lincoln City football supporters were leaving the ground at the same time and they were also witnesses to the unfolding events. Against his better judgement John allowed himself to be misdirected by the police on to a route unknown to him and not the usual one that he followed. The result was, his trailer hit a number of roundabout bollards as he negotiated the elongated load through the city centre. As he hit each object, the football supporters who had by now gathered en masse to watch, cheered lustily whenever a crunch was seen and heard. John was rightly indignant at his expertise and knowledge of the route being so blithely ignored by the local constabulary.

Whenever a heavy and awkward load was being transported any great distances, it often meant there would be a number of 'Black Gang' staff and steersmen plus mates to accompany it. Being on the road for the men meant that they had to have subsistence money with which to pay for their digs and out of pocket expenses. If it was a fairly large amount of money required, arrangements would be made for a money order to be sent to a post office en-route and a designated staff member would leave early to collect it. Bill Stephenson, a long time member of the Black Gang recalls a long large load run when such arrangements had been made and George Wrightson was nominated to collect it at the named post office. When Bill and the rest arrived at the rendezvous point, they found George stretched out on the grass verge, oblivious to all and sundry, drunk as a lord, They hauled him to his feet, threw him into the cab and pressed on. It was several hours before he was sober enough for him to play any part in the run.

Being a long distance lorry driver was by nature an occupation that kept drivers and their mates away from home for long periods of time with its well known consequences for a personal life. The problems of wives and children are well known, but there was also the lack of social life of the men involved. Many were members of darts and domino teams at various pubs and clubs in the area, and travelling away meant missing out on important matches in those two indoor 'sports'. Eighteen year old Freddy Thompson was given a job as a mate by Mr. Len once again after a chance meeting and was told on that same day to meet Jack Stout at Leeming Bar and act as his mate on a run to South Wales. He was picked up at the named spot and they set off for Wales. After a few miles Jack said, "Where are you stopping tonight Freddy?" Puzzled Freddy replied "At our first night stop further down the road I suppose" Jack Replied, "Well you might be lad but I'm sleeping at home tonight, I've got an important domino match on at the pub". On reaching Boroughbridge which is no more than fifteen miles from the depot, he parked up and set off to hitch a lift back to Northallerton. Non-plussed, Freddy did the same. They finally set off proper for Wales the following morning. In those early days of transport driving, hitch hiking back home was the norm for drivers and mates, there was no such thing as catching a train or bus or the funds with which to do it. Tom and Len realised that the men were working a flanker by parking up and hitching a lift home, so they changed the system When a load was parked relatively near the depot, George Percival was ordered to go an pick up the crew in a Morris Minor van and bring them home. The van had just two seats, one for the driver and one for the passenger, anyone else had to sit or lie in the back on the uncomfortable journey back to Northallerton. As much as the men disliked and thought this a trifle unfair, there is no doubt it saved a fair amount of money on subsistence.

In those days, pressure on the drivers and their mates to deliver the loads was almost non-stop. Len or Tom would always be asking why a certain load had not been delivered sooner, or being asked why they were late back at the depot. No sooner would a driver arrive back at the depot, he would be asked to take another load out. Artic driver Les Taylor recalls doing a double run carrying steel from Tees-side to Wales all within a twenty-four hour period with barely a break. On the third leg to Wales the fatigue began to get to him so on reaching Nottinghamshire he pulled into a large lay-by to settle down for some much needed sleep. He had no sooner closed his eyes, when the cab door opened and there stood Tom Sunter. "What are you doing lad!" were Tom's words. Les explained the situation and with a gruff order to "Don't take too long over it", Tom Sunter walked back to his Rolls Royce. To be fair Tom hadn't planned to look for Les; he had just been passing when he saw the wagon laid up in the lay-by.

Jim Fletcher was an irascible Sunter character who first joined the firm during the war and drove all manner of wagons including artics and then went on to drive the ballasted tractors. Jim was his own man and many who worked with him found out that trait through experience. Peter Clark recalls when he was acting as Jim's mate on a long load run and it was a run that taught him a lesson. That lesson was to never mess Jim Fletcher about. They were driving along at a steady pace when Jim, an inveterate pipe smoker handed Peter a gnarled bitten pipe and a pouch of rough-cut baccy, indicating that he, Peter should fill it for him. Peter decided that he couldn't be bothered to rub the baccy so he simply stuffed a load into the bowl and packed it as hard as he could then handed it to Jim. Jim lit up and sucked and sucked but it would not burn. After a couple of minutes he stopped and told Peter to go to the rear and steer the trailer around the forthcoming roundabout. It was only a small roundabout and it was pouring with rain. Puzzled as to why he was fussing about such a small roundabout, Peter got to the back and began steering while being soaked to the skin as the rain and the water from pools splashed on to him. As soon as they had negotiated the roundabout, Jim stopped the tractor to allow Peter to get off; he then accelerated away leaving his steersman stranded and soaking wet. Two very wet miles later Peter caught up with Jim who had parked and waited. On climbing into the cab, Jim quietly said, "You will fill my pipe properly next time won't you Peter?" On another occasion, Jim was on the outskirts of Leeds, being led by his escort, a policeman whom he knew very well, when he decided to stop and disappear into a nearby newsagents shop. The policeman who was further ahead came back and remonstrated with Jim for stopping and causing a back flow of traffic. Jim waited for the officer to have his say and then presented him with a packet of his favourite cigars and wished him a happy birthday. A much abashed but pleasantly surprised policeman waved Jim on and they restarted their journey.

Campbell Wardlaw QC was the solicitor who represented the company on their many legal cases. He was a strong and forceful advocate who defended his clients both Sunters and the individual with great tenacity and skill. Although he fought for the best result, he was sometimes exasperated beyond forbearance at times with some of the tenuous cases he had to fight. One such case involved a senior driver at Sunters. It was well know that almost all transport companies overloaded their vehicles and trailers to maximise their delivery tonnage and of course Sunters were no different. The driver who will remain nameless was travelling close to the town of Wetherby when the police who knew by experience when a vehicle was over laden flagged him down. They directed him to a public weighbridge at John Smith's Breweries at Tadcaster for a weighing. The driver knew he was over weight and refused to go on to the weigh bridge siting that if he did so it would mean crossing a tarmac footpath and there would be great danger that his vehicle would sink and cause some damage. An argument ensued and the result was the driver was charged by the police for not obeying a lawful police instruction and duly appeared in court. Campbell Wardlaw had to draw on every bit of his advocating skills to get the driver off the charge, but warned the company that he would be unwilling to defend any more such cases. Such cases as this and those of County Councils using the courts to claim compensation for damage to their roads (caused by the heavy loads) kept Campbell Wardlaw and the 'Legal Eagle' representatives of other haulage companies very busy indeed.

Although many of the stories about Sunters are amusing, there were four that ended in tragedy. The first was during the war that involved John Robinson mentioned earlier in the story. The second tragedy happened in May of 1961, when the Mountaineer KVN 604 driven by 'Coconut Joe' Whillis was involved in a fatal accident at Shap in Cumbria, when it was in collision with a gravel lorry. The impact by the gravel lorry into the Mountaineer was so severe that the front axle of the Sunter's wagon was pushed under the crushed cab. The impact also severely injured the gravel lorry driver who later died in hospital. Bill Jemison who was backing up Coconut Joe with a 6x4 Atkinson had his wagon and the load pushed back a number of yards after the impact. The third accident happened when an artic loaded with steel was being driven through Micklefield. The driver who will remain nameless was travelling down the hill into the town centre, when he was compelled to brake sharply for a dog and its owner who crossed in front of his vehicle. The sudden force of the braking, caused the load of steel to rapidly shunt forward at the same time sending the vehicle off the side of the road, the load crushing the driver to death. The fourth accident happened in Darrington near Ferryhill. A passing tanker burst a tyre and collided with the Sunter's vehicle. The tanker driver quickly escaped from his cab, but the tanker rolled over and crushed him to death. It was the tanker driver's last run before his retirement. There was a fifth accident but fortunately it was not quite so serious. Artic driver Stan Sygmuta was delivering a load of pipes when he had cause to brake sharply while travelling between Northallerton and Darlington. The load shunted toward the cab causing one of the pipes to slide forward which pinned him to the windscreen of his vehicle. Fortunately the speed of the vehicle was not great and this probably saved his life, although he did suffer slight neck injuries. The constant factor in the latter three stories was that all three drivers had been driving the Atkinson 150 artic Reg. No. EVN 333C. After the last accident, Peter Sunter, not wishing to tempt fate any further, got rid of the vehicle.

The Four Main Sunter Trailers

The Mountaineer with 'Sunter Brothers' trailer.

The Super Constructor with Sunter Brothers Scheuler trailer

The Mountaineer with crane 90 ton suspension 'Sunter Brothers' trailer.

The Rotinoff with Sunter Brothers Crane trailer.

...at the Depot

No matter where a load had to be delivered and no matter how large, it could not move without the assistance or say so of the depot staff. From the engineers in the servicing bays to the bevy of girls in the office and of course - Joe Taylor, before anything could start, the paperwork had to be organised and prepared. One of the many motor fitters/engineers at the depot was Michael Piechcohi an ex patriot Pole who came to England after serving with the Free Polish Army in the Middle East and Italy. Michael was a first class motor engineer who never ever let a problem defeat him. His standard mantra in his Polish/English accent when presented with a mechanical problem was, "Let it run, I fix it"

Michael started life in Northallerton with a very poor grasp of the English language and by living very frugally in a single room in a shed cum house at the Boroughbridge Road depot, but he never complained and simply got on with life. John Robinson felt compassion for Michael and would often invite him over to his home for the occasional meal and to allow him the use of a hot bath. Mike eventually married and raised a family in Northallerton, but his love for Poland never diminished. His pride and gratitude at being allowed to live as a free man in England meant a great deal to him and he never hid that gratitude. There is a story about Mike and a disgruntled Sunter employee who shall remain anonymous who began a long and foul-mouthed diatribe against the Royal Family. Mike rounded on him and told him in no uncertain fashion that he should be thankful that he lived in a country as free as England with a Queen who was so well respected. He finished off by telling the chap that if he didn't like England, he should try living in Poland then he might not complain quite so much. David Murhpy who also worked in the maintenance shop, can vouch for Michael Piochoci's fiery disposition but found him to be a man of principle and decency. When Poland broke free from Russia in the 1970s, Michael finally got his wish to visit the free country of his birth. He had not seen Poland for more than forty years, but returned very quickly. To help him on his way, several close friends chipped in to help with the fare. It was a most generous gesture that was truly appreciated by Michael.

It goes without saying that vehicle purchasing is an expensive business and as such, it was not always a viable thing to buy new models. To reduce costs, Sunters would sometimes buy second hand vehicles to supplement the fleet. The company that Len dealt with for these acquisitions was Tex Cross Road Commercials of Guilderson near Leeds. On receipt of a second hand unit, the bodywork would be prepared for Sunters livery and when it was ready, it would then join the fleet. Ted Daynes a former artic driver recalls on at least three occasions being invited by Lenny to take his old number plate and attach it to the 'new' unit. Obviously, the registering of vehicles was not quite so strict then as it is today. On one occasion when Sunters had taken delivery of a reconstructed tractor, the paint finishers stripped away the top layer of paint only to discover underneath, the red and grey livery of Sunters. They had re-bought one of their old tractor units. The discovery produced some choice expletives from Mr. Len, but he laughed it off in the end. To reduce costs in repairs and renewal of spares for the fleet, the fitters at the depot would mend and make do with a lot of local refinements. When Phil Braithwaite was an artic driver of AEC Mammoth Major LPY 256, the rear mudguards of his artic unit were constructed from a section of corrugated sheeting taken from a wartime Anderson shelter. The corrugated sheeting was strong, durable and it served the purpose perfectly and showed a mark of the ingenuity by the maintenance staff.

Once a tractor unit had seen the best of its days, it was sold off to who ever would buy it and one such ballasted tractor ended up at a breakdown garage a few miles from Sunter's depot. Scammel Super Constructor 447 DPY that began its life as a brand new vehicle with Sunters, ended up at Topcliffe Garage on the Topcliffe Road near Northallerton as a heavy breakdown and recovery truck. The proprietor Richard Lawley had the vehicle painted in the blue and white livery of his company and it served valiantly for many years until being sold off once more, this time to a collector David Weedon of York who is currently repainting it in Sunter's colours.

Topcliffe Garage eventually became Topcliffe Crane Hire and their business prospered by obtaining craneage contracts with many of the local firms including ICI. The use of cranes was an important part of load preparation for Sunters and they too employed the cranes from Lawley's of Topcliffe. Preparing trailers for specific loads was a time consuming, heavy and awkward task and those tasks always fell to Sunter's Black Gang. It was a complicated affair re-arranging the various sections of trailers and almost always there was need for a crane to move and hoist trailer sections into position. Topcliffe Crane Hire at Topcliffe Road was the company that was regularly brought in to do lifting. Ralph Lawley began his crane hire business in the 1960s with two-second hand RAF Coles cranes, one of five-tons capacity and the other at ten tons. By the later 1970s he had acquired a fifteen-ton hydraulic crane that was in great demand around the local area. His expertise was often hired by Sunters to help with the moving of trailers and heavy equipment. Although craning is a difficult and precise job with implicit safety precautions, the Black Gang in the yard would often try to coax Richard Lawley into moving weights either far in excess of the cranes capacity or a weight too greater distance from the crane base. This could have been extremely dangerous and if it had not been for the intervention of Philip Braithwaite the yard foreman who knew about crane weights and tolerances, accidents were avoided.

...and of Mr. Len.

On the death of his brother Tom and the merging with United Transport, Len Sunter took over the reins of the company and the extra burden of responsibility placed on him made for some interesting and hilarious statements and memorable episodes. Len, forever the Dalesman, with none of the refinements adopted by his brother was bluff, short on temper, generous and mean in equal measure, magnanimous and at times unintentionally funny. All this, coupled with his Dales speak dialect, made Len Sunter an endearingly friendly man. No history of the company would be complete without a mention of just a few of the many hundreds of anecdotes that surround this earthy character. Mr. Len as he was always called by one and all, was first and foremost a 'Sacker' and a 'Reinstater'. There is hardly a person who ever has been employed by Sunters who has not been threatened with the sack or sacked and then reinstated by that volatile boss.

On one occasion Len told one worker in straightforward high decibel language peppered with several F words to "Get off the 'Fourxxxxing!' site, thoo's sacked!" At that, the rest of the gang began pleading with Len saying, "You know Mr. Len, now he's gone we'll have to get a young lad from the Labour Exchange to take his place, and besides, what about his kids?" On hearing that the sacked worker had a family, Len would often relent and say "Get tha' self back on the site and don't do it again" This scenario happened in a variety of ways throughout Len's tenure as the boss. One employee actually left the site and set off to the pub only to be caught up by Len in his car to be told to get in and to be taken back to work. Len would often sack a man who would duly leave the site as ordered and not appear for sometime. A chance meeting between the two, usually during the day in the 'Sunter's pub, namely, the North Riding would end up by Len saying "Why aren't thoo at work lad?" When he was told that he had been given the sack, Len would often say, "Get tha self back to the yard and get to work". Although Len could be generous, he could at times be described as they say in Yorkshire a bit 'near' (miserly) as almost always when he was a buying a drink for the lads; he would only offer half a pint. However in his defence, there were scores of potential employees for whom he might have to buy beer. Bill Stephenson a former Black Gang member recalls another tale of his reluctance to part with the 'brass' when he was once called to Len's bungalow on Brompton Road and to bring a flat back wagon from the yard with him. On his arrival Bill was asked by Len to throw a huge heap of hedge and rose cuttings plus general garden detritus on to the back of the truck and to get rid of them. He then offered Bill a sixpenny piece with the instruction "Get tha self a drink".

Len was not taken by the modern hairstyle of the 1960s and the young apprentices such as Peter Broughton, who wore their hair almost to their shoulders, would regularly be told to get a haircut and given a 2/- piece to have the job done. Phoning in to the depot with problems was a chance a driver had to take whenever Len might answer the phone. If a driver phoned in from some distant part of the country to tell Len that he had been held up by snow, fog or some other weather condition, more often than not he would received the sharp reply "Well it's not snowing/foggy in Northallerton".

In the early days of the business Len Sunter did his share of mating on long hauls and John Robinson recalls a trip in a Bedford that 'sported' rod-brakes, which entailed loading up at Teesside and passing through Thirsk. It was almost night time by the time they reached Thirsk, so Len made the suggestion that they 'walk' to Sutton Under Whitestonecliffe, a village a few miles from Thirsk to where his sister-in law-lived. There they spent the night ready for an early start. The return journey to Thirsk to where the wagon was parked turned into a bizarre trip. Len acquired a bike from somewhere and said that he would ride a couple of miles, leave the bike in a hedge back for John to pick up and then walk on a couple of miles until he was caught up by John on the bike. This way it would be quicker and would reduce the walking time. Len being the boss took the first ride of the bike and pedalled off, while John trudged off on foot. After a couple of miles, Len laid the bike by the side of the road and set off walking. In the meanwhile John caught up, found the bike, pedalled away until he caught up with Len and then it was his turn to lay down the bike and walk. According to John, this odd leapfrog system apparently worked and gave both of them a rest from walking and according to John was a speedier way of reaching their destination. To this day John thinks that he spent a lot of his 'walking time' sitting in the hedgeback waiting for his turn on the bike.

With his experience of mating, Len knew the ropes and it might be said he also knew the fiddles and so by those experiences was on the look out for dodgy expense sheet returns. Many an expense sheet would be torn up with the exhortation, "Thoo can't put in an expense sheet like that lad! sort it out!" The culprit would make out another sheet exactly like the first one and Len would say "That's better!" He once issued an instruction that under no circumstances drivers were to give lifts to anyone who appeared to be a dubious looking character, e.g. tramps etc, but unfortunately his order backfired on him one day. Whilst trying to thumb a lift back to the depot dressed in an old overcoat with a length of 'billy-band' tied round his waist and for all the world looking like a tramp, he was approached by one of his own wagons. Len flagged him down, but the driver resolutely refused to stop. When Len eventually got back to the depot he was incandescent with rage and for days hunted the driver who had left him behind, but the crafty driver managed to keep out of his way until things had calmed down, his excuse for not picking up Len was that he looked like a tramp, even though he knew perfectly well who it was but simply obeyed orders.

It was a well known fact that when on the road, the men liked to partake of the odd alcoholic beverage, although it was strictly against the rules. John 'Ginger' Dale a mate/black gang member who cheerfully admits to being demobbed from the Military Detention Centre of Colchester on completion of his army national service (six months late) recalls a run when more than a few beverages had been consumed. He was acting as mate to Harry Burns when they were both returning from Teesside via the small town of Yarm and happened to pass near their favourite hostelry. As it was almost lunch time-11am? they stopped. Four hours and several pints later they staggered back to the wagon. Harry Burns was beyond the call and immediately fell asleep in the mate's position in the cab. Nothing that Ginger could do would make Harry attempt to drive. Ginger who was able to drive but was not a registered driver with the company decided to take the outfit back to the depot himself even though he was only marginally less 'sleepy' than Harry Burns. On arriving at Brompton a mile from Northallerton, Ginger stopped to try and get Harry to drive the rig into the yard, but slumbering Harry refused. Ginger carried on and on entering the yard, who was there waiting for them but Mr. Len. In a raging flurry of expletives and colloquial language, Len rounded on Harry Burns and demanded to know why he had let a non-qualified driver, drive a £24,000 tractor unit. On seeing that Harry was in no fit state to reply he sacked him on the spot. He then turned his anger on Ginger and suspended him for two weeks forthwith. Ginger promptly left the site and in the next few days realising that he would not ever get back to Sunters, he went job hunting. After not having much success he drifted into 'Sunter's pub' and there was Mr. Len standing at the bar. 'What's tha doin' ere ?' demanded Len. 'You suspended me Mr. Len and I don't think I'll ever get back with you' came the reply. 'Get thisen back to work lad!' Len responded. So that was that, Ginger carried on working as if nothing had ever happened.

Blunt and pithy advice to his staff was never in short supply from Len Sunter. On one occasion a driver phoned in to say that he had run out of coolant and that there was no water supply near by. With his well-known exasperation and short temper, Len bawled down the telephone with the words, "Piss in the radiator lad!" What he really meant in his own earthy way, was, that the driver should use his initiative and get some water one way or another. All, on the road staff would routinely add an extra few hours to their time sheets each week as a sort of personal bonus. If this transgression was spotted it would be refused and no payment made. Almost always the drivers would then double the hours in the next week's claim and usually get it back that way. In its way, it was a form of 'Catch as catch can' While on honeymoon with his wife Ann, George Percival received a phone call from Len more or less ordering him to call at Dereham to collect spare parts for a trailer which were needed as soon as possible. Honeymoon or not, work had to go on and so George had to comply. Another time when George had been sent to Leeds to collect spare parts, he was away for much longer than Len cared. On his return he was asked by an irritable Mr. Len "Where's thoo been" George told him that there had been a queue at the spare parts dept. Len's reply was "A queue! Didn't tha tell them that you were from Sunters!?" Although this may have sounded a bit pretentious, this was code for gratuity. The suppliers knew that Sunter Brothers were 'generous' when they required special treatment?

Whenever work was slack, drivers, mates and the Black Gang were expected to find something useful to do. This meant having a yard brush, a paintbrush; a spanner or oilcan in their hands. Maintenance of the yard and equipment was an ongoing business and Len always insisted on his employees being 'gainfully' employed and was forever harrying and chasing the men if were not looking busy. Being chased and watched led to the 'act of looking busy' into the 'art of looking busy'. Men would

Social Occasions

*A presentation of Carriage Clocks
at the Golden Lion Hotel, Northallerton for 25 Year's service.
Jim Fletcher - Les Taylor - Phil Braithwaite - Jack Stout - Len Sunter - Sybil Sunter
John Robinson - Jack Thompson - Tony Swann*

*A Sunter's
Christmas
party
in
Northallerton
Town Hall.*

*Len Sunter
with a group of his employees
at the Golden Lion Hotel*

pretend to be doing all sorts of jobs whenever Len was around, but the moment his back was turned.

In the early years, Sunters always awarded their employees for their loyalty. Whenever an employee reached 25 years service, he or she would be presented with an engraved carriage clock as a mark of thanks and gratitude by the company. Len usually made the presentations during a pleasant and friendly dinner function at the Golden Lion Hotel in Northallerton. Likewise, the Christmas dinner was held in the Town Hall with plenty of liquid refreshments laid on. These gestures were greatly appreciated by the employees and helped to cement a family atmosphere within the company.

A book could be written about the pithy sayings, earthy manner and unending faux pas of Len Sunter. There is hardly a former employee who does not have a goodly store of 'Sunteresque' tales of Mr Len' Almost all are humorous in nature and even the ones that were serious had their amusing side. Fall-outs he had by the score, but to a man, all agree that above all, Len never held a grudge and when it was forgotten, it remained forgotten. For all his glaring faults and rough hewn manner, almost everyone who came within range of his voice and direct manner held an everlasting affection for this quick tempered but good natured Dalesman.

Record Breakers

High Wide and Mighty were the loads that Sunters Heavy Haulage carried nation wide and later around the world, but High Wide and Awkward could be another way of describing them. The Bradwell move was a record breaker in its own right and was exceptionally awkward in its delivery and installation. Without doubt it set the company on the way to being near the top of the league of heavy hauliers, but at least on two other occasions the company carried official record-breaking loads that eventually entered the record books. The first of those two loads was one that was not particularly heavy by later Sunter standards, weighing in at a mere 285 tons, but it was long - very long. It stretched 221 feet and had a width of 17ft.4 ins. Adding to the difficulties, the load had to be taken along a winding route through the built up suburbs of Billingham and Tees-side. The load being carried was a nitric acid column from Head Wrightson of Thornaby destined for the ICI Agricultural Division industrial complex and just one of scores of such columns to be installed there over the next few months. The date was Sunday 25th of March 1984 and the time of the haul was a sleepy 5.30am. This didn't deter the public's interest. Long before the nitric acid column made its first move, several hundreds of sightseers both young and old had gathered in the cold morning air to witness this spectacular scene.

The nitric acid container was to be towed by Sunter's French built Tractomas driven by Albert Lowes and by two German built Mercedes Titans, driven by Malcolm Johnson and Alan Massie and carried on two Nicolas hydraulic suspension trailers. These two trailers had a configuration of 18 axles borne on 184 wheels and initially had to be driven up a relatively steep gradient on the first leg of its journey. The length of the load was such that it required the 'street furniture' e.g. lampposts, road directions signs to be uprooted and carted clear of the route and roundabouts bisected. The cost alone for the furniture and roundabout removal came to a cool £20,000. Despite all the problems and cost, the load was delivered and sited within the time limits allowed. Overhead telephone cables and plant were particular problems for both the haulier and the company. Dennis Goode of Maltby near Middlesbrough was the area liaison officer for the Post Office later British Telecom, and it was his job to protect all telephone installation on the route taken by such large loads. Not only was his job to protect company property, but he was also expected to inform all subscribers that their services were likely to be interrupted and for how long. When he had done that he had to calculate the likely costs to the carrier for Telecom's disruption of services. Advance notice had to be given to all concerned and this was often some eighteen months and on occasion two years before the load was moved.

There was always an official route planned by the Ministry of Transport but these were often ignored. Not through bloody mindedness, but due to road works that had not even been thought of when the route was planned or as often as not the specifications of the load had been altered, i.e. too high, too long/wide/heavy/ and in load in tons per wheel. On one occasion Dennis remembers a wide heavy load having to be re-diverted through the North Yorkshire villages of Thornton-le-Moor and Thornton-le-Beans. These two tiny villages each with a narrow winding main street and a population that is numbered in the hundreds, had to witness a Sunters heavy tractor and monster load lumbering its way past their cottages. Dennis also had to take in the time taken for a load to pass a given point on the route and in some instances it took upwards of three hours for the monster load to simply negotiate a corner! For Dennis Goode they were interesting times.

In a previous operation, ICI hired Sunters for another gigantic move and as part of the delivery process bought a row of terraced houses which intruded en route, re-housed the residents, knocked the dwellings down and built a huge tar-mac area just to allow the tractor unit and load a turning point. Such is the way of moving such unwieldy and large loads on the Queen's Highway.

The second record load was captured by the television cameras on the BBC Television programme 'Jim'll Fix It' In mid 1984, eleven-year-old schoolboy Paul Campbell of Allerton in West Yorkshire along with his school classmates, was given the task of writing a letter to that garrulous TV personality Jimmy Savile asking if he could fix it for him drive an articulated lorry. The letters in the first instance were a writing exercise as part of their class work and none of the pupils thought anymore of their efforts. Unbeknown to them, the school posted all the letters to the producer of the BBC programme. Several months later a letter reached the Campbell household informing them that Paul's request to drive an articulated lorry was to be fulfilled. Unbeknown also to Paul, Jimmy Savile had 'upgraded' his request from driving an articulated lorry to driving a record-breaking load for Scott Lithgow of Glasgow and Sunters Heavy Haulage of Northallerton. Scott Lithgow was an offshore oil company that specialised in constructing all manner of modules for the booming North Sea oil industry. Under construction at Redpath Offshore at Teesside (sister company to Scott Lithgow) was an accommodation module with dimensions that were awe-inspiring. It was 106ft wide, 73ft long, and 55ft high and weighed in at 1,305 tonnes and was in the final stages for its move to Glasgow for completion. This was the load that Paul was going to move with a little help from Sunters and a posse of heavy tractors. However, the first move for the module was a six day sea journey by barge to the Clyde. The first part of the move was organised and controlled by Peter Sunter of Sunters-ITM (International Transport Management). The sea trip was a minor detail in the grand scheme of things; its arrival at Clydeside was the start of the real problems and headaches. The chief problem was that the load had to be moved along a public road and the public road to be used was not 106ft wide. It was decided that an artificial road would have to be constructed and laid parallel to the exiting road to accommodate half of the width of the module. Not only was an extra road required, all the signs and barriers of the original road had to be removed.

At this juncture it is worth introducing all those who played a prominent part in the drama. There was Peter Sunter the Boss of the company, on push and pull were Albert Lowes, Alan Massie. Malcolm Johnson and Ken Bickerton, ballasted tractor drivers to a man. Albert was in control of the French built Tracotmas,

*Albert Lowes
and
Paul Cambell
in the Tractomas*

Paul Cambell

A group of Sunter Lads who were on the record breaking Billingham run.
Back row: Ken Thompson - Peter Broughton - Ken Bickerton - Malcolm Johnson - Bob Lincoln
Front row: Gordon Shepherd - Ivan Costick - John Garret - Albert Lowes

Steady as she goes
Coz' Costick keeping the load level

Bill Stephenson of the Black Gang

Malcolm a Titan Mercedes V, Ken a Titan Mercedes, and Alan in control of a Volvo F. In support of the move were Foreman Steersman Ivan Costick who and steersmen George Wrightson, John Garrett, Ken Thomas and Michael Tobin, with John Wood overseeing the levelling of the trailers. David Taylor, a calm cool taciturn character who had taken charge of scores of similar heavy moves was in control of the whole operation. Paul, who is now twenty four years old, remembers that event with a mixture of pride and a little embarrassment.

Alan Massie was what you might say in another record breaking event of a sort. Both he and John Robinson travelled to Scammel's to collect the very first new Contractor TPY 675H. With them they took a pre-decimal cheque to the value of £10,500.10/- to pay for it. This was in the days when cash on the nail or a cheque were the preferred ways of paying and no doubt attracted a fair bit of discount as a result. That sort of deal is hardly heard of today with electronic banking and cash/cheque payments.

As the late 1970s and early 1980s arrived, the interest in 'Record breaking' became more or less academic within the industry. With the advent of oil within the UK and quantum leap in the size and weight of modules for that industry, huge loads in size and weight were rarely mentioned. However, heavy moves were still for the asking for Sunters at the start of the 1980s and they took full advantage of them. Three loads in particular were worthy of note all using the Nicolas trailers. The Nicolas modular trailers were exceptionally versatile as individual units may be coupled end-to-end or side-by-side. Connections on the hydraulic system are also variable so as to match the geometry of the trailer assembly and to provide three-point support with the broadest possible base in the triangle. Regardless of trailer size, steering beans can be fitted allowing accurate alignment and positioning of loads by utilising double acting steering cylinders. Sunters also facilitated loads by the use of their hydraulic jack system for levelling loads to the required height for the trailer to be placed underneath. This method saved a great number of man-hours, thus speeding up the entire job.

An example of that versatility was provided when a 2600 tonne capacity trailer was positioned under a 2,000 tonne production module prior to load-out at William Press Systems Ltd on Tyneside. The hydraulic suspension of the Nicolas trailer ensured a uniform load distribution of something in the order of 5.5 tonnes per square metre. With its-self steering and self-stabilising capability, the trailers were proving their value. Other examples were, three Scammel Contractors and a Titan hauled a 1,200 tons module out of Whessoe Darlington and a couple of months later three Contractors, the Tractomas and Titan were involved in moving a module weighing in at a little over 3,000 tonnes on the Cleveland bridge site at Port Clarence. The trailers bearing the weight on no fewer than 1,088 tyres.

Among all the record breaking moves and load-outs, there was a steady flow of interesting and slightly different but lighter loads moved by the heavy tractors and artics, namely-steam locomotives, carriages and continental tramcars. Moving steam locos was nothing new for Sunters, but the celebrity of the moves in the 1980s was what made them different. Perhaps the most famous was the loading and carrying of record breaking steam engine Mallard which was moved from Clapham to Stewart's Lane railhead for transportation by the natural means i.e. rail to York. The loco was carried on an eight axled 64 wheeled trailer and pulled by a Contractor. Several other smaller locos were also carried during this period, which included a replica of Stevenson's Rocket and luxury carriages of the Orient Express. On reading of the transportation of locos by road, an indignant motorist wrote a letter to the national press complaining that carrying railway engines by road amounted to stupidity if not sacrilege. There was one steam loco however whose carriage by road could not have been described as sacrilegious. This engine was the British built 100 tonne black 8-6-0 loco that had a gauge some two feet wider than the standard gauge of Britain's railways. The locomotive was presented to the people of Great Britain by the Republic of China People's Railway. This engine is now in situ at the National Rail Museum, York and dwarfs the massive Evening Star loco by several feet in length, width and height. Other engine carried by Sunters could have travelled by rail, as their gauge was standard, although their ageing moving parts may not have been able stand up to the pounding of the wheels on the rails.

Another interesting load for Sunters was the moving of three large Stothert & Pitt 7 ton DD2 quay cranes from Alexandra Dock to the King George Dock in Hull. As cranes go, 7 tons may not seem to be a heavy lifting capacity, but these cranes towered to an overall height of 130ft! The one mile move for each crane took place over a ten day period that entailed negotiating several tight corners with a clearance of less than four inches, a 1-28 slope and the Corporation Road roundabout. A self-steering 40ft wheeled trailer was used with a Volvo pulling and the Tractomas pushing. Special jacking equipment was made by the Hull port and estuary engineers Central Workshops to facilitate the move. The jacks allowed the crane to be raised sufficiently high enough for it to be lowered onto the trailers. With the usual Sunter's professionalism, the moves went without a hitch, but Peter confesses to having a few minor nightmares about the move.

In many ways those times were the highs for the company. As 1985 receded, the staff from the offices to the workshops and the drivers and mates, got the feeling that things were not well with the company. There was a slow down in work and a slow down in morale. Something had to give.

Prior to leaving the business, Peter Sunter had the difficult job of closing down Wynn's operations in Wales and other areas. Wynns was a company that had been in the haulage business for more than a hundred years and they were having precisely the same problems as Sunters were experiencing. In the early years Wynns who were based at Newport in Gwent were in the perfect place for the industries that were in that part of Wales. The new generation of industries being built e.g. steelworks, oil consortiums, petro/chemical industries were being sited at the western reaches of South Wales. For Wynns the final blow came when the Severn Bridge was down graded to a maximum loading of 38 tons, which then entailed travelling a tortuous route down to Worcester and the M4 Motorway to reach South Wales. That ruling spelt the death knell for the company. Peter then had to tackle the tasteless job of closing down the depots at Newport, Gwent, Cardiff (tankers) Chasetown and Old Trafford in Manchester. It was tasteless inasmuch that he had to make 240 people redundant, but he did manage to keep 92 people in work. While he was in the process of making those people redundant he was told that he must change his car for a new model. Peter refused point blank saying that he could not tell men that they no longer had a job when he had a brand new car parked outside his office. Despite Peter's distaste for that facet of the job, it was one that had to be done and he realised that being in such a position of management there was no easy way.

Nemesis

The story of Sunters in essence began in the reign of Queen Victoria with the marriage of George and Alice and the struggles and hardships over the years were many. Tom, Len and Joss Sunter built up the company through sheer hard work and on the part of Tom an inborn business sense and a willingness to take a chance and face a challenge, which he did in a variety of ways. With the death of Tom and the absorption of the company into Bulwark United Transport, the nature of the company changed markedly. The demands of the heavy transport market, technology and the boom in the UK oil industry placed new demands on the company. Many of those demands were met and the company prospered especially under the management of Peter. As Peter has explained, with the hierarchy of BUT remote from Northallerton and not having that direct connection, the company began to slide. He had left Northallerton in the late 1970s for a management job in the Midlands and finally left the consortium at the end of 1982. The heart had been taken out of his desire to stay with the business. He had realised that Sunters was going down hill and had warned that within a few short years the company would have to close if they didn't change. Things went from bad to worse and Henry Wood, the Operations Manager, could not prevent the slide of the company to the point of no return. The site at Boroughbridge Road in Northallerton was too remote from where the real business that was being conducted in the mid 1980s. It was imperative that their operations should move to where the work actually was, e.g. Tees-side. In short they were in the wrong place. In the very early 1980s Sunters had plenty of orders especially with Head Wrightson and Foster-Wheeler and were working at a fairly full capacity, but even the road crews and the staff in the office were beginning to realise that all was not well.

Friday the 16th of May 1986 was Black Friday for Sunter's employees. Wynns, Wrekin Roadways and Econofreight all merged to form a single company under the banner of Econofreight United Transport (EUT), which in turn was owned by United Transport, which in turn was a subsidiary of BET and Transport Development Group. PLC, the Managing Director being Tom Llewellyn. All the named companies in the take over operated under their own named companies but were transposed to the wearing of the blue and white livery logo and name of Econofreight. Gone from the highways were the distinctive colours of grey and red that had emblazoned the Sunter fleet for so many years and gone also, was that famous name. This to all intents and purposes spelt the end of this once giant of the heavy haulage industry. It was nemesis of a distinctive family connected business.

The transfer to Econofreight may have been carried out professionally from the business angle but from the human aspect and to the manner in which some staff members at Sunter's depot on Boroughbridge Road, Northallerton got to know their employment destinies was less than subtle. Drivers and mates arriving at the depot to collect their wage and enquire about the next run on that fateful Friday in May, were met by the transport manager with their wage packets and the instruction that the depot was closing and they were now working for Econofreight. The ones who happened to be on the continent were informed by telephone leaving them somewhat stranded. Almost to a man, they thought that the whole business of transfer to Econofreight had been handled very badly and with very little thought. The depot at Northallerton was closed and sold off as part of the deal. One big regret for Peter Sunter other than the disappearance of the family name, was the selling of the land on which the company had stood for so many years. The site is now a housing estate and sad to say, there is not so much as a reference in the form of a lane or avenue to the once proud Sunter name. The last load out of a wet and soggy Boroughbridge Road depot was a Sunter Super Contractor in the colours of Wynn's Transport leading a trailer and a structure load both with Sunter and Econofreight colours. So ended sixty years of haulage and social history, but the memories and the name will live on.

The names of some of former staff members employed by
Sunter Brothers.

Adams.S.	Dale.J.	Jobling.V.	Shepherd G.
Adams.T.	Daynes.E...	Jobling.R.	Simpson.K.
Alderson.J.	Dodsworth.J.	Johns.O.	Stead.A.
Allsop.H.	Dodsworth. P.	Johnson.L.	Stephenson.W.
Barton.J.	Emms.J.	Johnson.M.	Stevenson.E.
Beasley.E.	Fletcher.R.	Kendall.J.	Stevenson.G.
Bellerby.	Fletcher.R.	Leng.A.	Stout..J.
Bickerton.K.	Foulds.D.	Lincoln.R.	Stubbs.R.
Bland. I.	Fox.A.	Lowes.A.	Sunter.P.
Braithwaite. P.J.	Fraser. M	Massie.A.	Swann.T.
Braithwaite.G.	Fraser. J.	Massey.	Sygmuta.S.
Braithwite.P.	French.K.	McHugh.G.	Taylor.D.
Brandley.R.	Garrett.J.	McLaughlin.P.	Taylor.J.
Brass.H.	Garthwaite. N	Meeks.R	Taylor.I..
Brass.N.	Gibson.D.	Murphy. C.	Thompson.F.
Broughton.P.	Gill.M.	Murphy.D.	Thompson.J.
Brown.B	Godfrey.	Neill.M.	Thompson.T.
Brown.T..	Goulding.J.	Oldfield.P	Wadowski.T.
Burns.H.	Gregory.F.	Percival.G.	Wake.C.
Carter.N.	Hanner.B.	Perry.W.	Walker.A.
Caven.W.	Hart.G.	Pickersgill.E.	Ward.D.
Caygill..A	Helm.R.	Pickard.R.	Warren.D.
Christon.P.	Henderson.J.	Piechochi.M	Watts.G.
Clark.C.	Hobson.J.	Pooley.A	Whillis.J.
Clark.P.	Hudson.T.	Port.A.	H.Wood
Clark.R.S.	Humphrey.B.	Pratt.R.	Wood.T.
Claxton.J.	Hunt. A	Prior..L	Wooler.C.
Cleary.A	Husted.E.	Rigg.	Wright.J.
Clemmett.P.	Hutchinson.B.	Robinson.J.A.	Wrightson.G.
Costick.I.	Jackson.H.	Robinson.T	Wrightson.G. (Jnr)
Coultman.R.	Jemison.W.	Rose.H.	Wynn.H.
Coulthard..C	Jobling.A	Scaife.T.	
Cree.J.	Jobling.P.	Sharp.R.	

Apologies for those who are not listed.

What happened to...

It is now close on twenty years since the name Sunter disappeared from the town of Northallerton and twenty years since the last load left a rain sodden Boroughbridge Road Depot. Gone are the heavy tractors units, artics, multi wheeled trailers and gone also are the men and women who gave the company its heartbeat. The depot is now a modern housing estate with nary a lane, drive or street given the name Sunter to remind one and all of that once proud company. The name is no more. The business name of Sunter is no more, but what of the men and women who over the years worked for this high profile transport company, without which it could never have functioned. Here are some of the names of that disparate band of people with the briefest of résumés about them.

John Robinson. Senior driver and employee retired some years before the company's demise, and now lives in retirement in Romanby but still manages to do the occasional medium distance mating runs with Bill Jemison.

Bill Jemison is retired but still manages to drive a light wagon with John Robinson acting as his mate. Bill is currently recovering from an 'internal plumbing job' at the hospital.

Philip Braithwaite (Senior) Phil is now retired and lives in Romanby, where he keeps his garden and works for the church.

Les Taylor lives in quiet retirement in Northallerton.

Jock Fraser lives with his partner in Newton le Willows.

Ken Simpson lives in retirement at Colburn.

Ted Daynes lives in retirement with his Swiss born wife and her music in Thirsk.

Albert Lowes lives in Romanby and spends four winter months of the year soaking up the sun in Spain.

David Murphy is a motor fitter with the North Yorkshire Fire & Rescue Services.

Michael Piechochi died in August 2000 at the age of 86.

Peter Clemmett is a small holding farmer at Yarm.

Bill Stephenson retired in May 2000 as Head Porter of the Friarage Hospital after almost twenty years of preventing it from coming to a standstill.

Ivan Costick for so long under the eye of Head Porter Bill, is still portering away at the Friarage Hospital.

Joe Taylor died in February 2001.

David Taylor lives in Morton on Swale.

Phil Braithwaite (Junior) lives in Otterington and still works in heavy transport.

Bob Fletcher lives at Ripon and is still trucking.

Peter Clark lives in Northallerton but is currently off work due to injury.

Peter Broughton lives in Northallerton and works as a freelance driver with Econofreight.

Gordon Shepherd lives in retirement in Brompton.

John Garret lives in Northallerton and is a freelance driver.

Terry Thompson is still in the haulage business, but at the moment seems to be on a serial injury list.

John 'Ginger' Dale lives in Northallerton and frequents the Working Men's Club with other Sunter's men.

Paddy McLauchlin lives in Brompton and accompanies Ginger at the club.

Roy Brandley lives in Northallerton and works and is employed still in the heavy haulage industry.

Alan Massie lives in Northallerton and is a heavy haulage driver for Econofreight.

Ken Bickerton is now employed by the Northallerton Council.

Roy Pickard now works in the maintenance workshops for Walter Thompson Builders.

Celia Coulthard (Fawcett) lives in Northalleton and works for the Northern Echo.

Pam Turner (Crow) lives in Northallerton and works in the Wine Shop in the High Street.

Barbara Adams works for the North Yorks. County Library.

Heather Brass works as a cleaner at the path lab Friarage Hospital Northallerton.

Peter and Vernon Jobling are both retired but work part time as taxi drivers.

Nick Carter lives in Northallerton and uses the Working Men's Club.

Albert Pooley is retired and does likewise.

Arthur (Bandit) Cleary died in 2000.

John Henderson lives in retirement in Northallerton after working for the National Rail Museum York.

George Percival is retired and now lives in Darlington.

...and the **Sunter** family?

Margaret Sunter Tom's widow lives in Richmond

Audrey Sunter Joseph's widow lives in Richmond.

Rosa (Sunter) **Laurie** lives in Gunnerside near where the family was born and raised.

Peter Sunter the last 'Family Boss' of the company lives with his wife Christine in Northallerton and now runs 'Transcargo' his own heavy haul consultancy and has many overseas connections.

A
Gallery
of
Character
Snapshots

Ceila (Fawcett) Coulthard

Janet (Crow) Turner

Heather Brass

Sue (Blades) Fraser

Lesley (George) Murphy

Barbara Adams

Alan Joblings

Albert Lowes

Gordon Braithwaite

Peter Sunter

Des Gibson

John Dodsworth

Tommy Brown

John Garrett

Stan Sygmuta

Peter Broughton

Philip Braithwaite (jnr)

Philip Braithwaite (snr)

Paddy McLaughlin

John Dale

Arthur Cleary

Jack Emms

Nick Carter

Jim Fletcher

Peter Clark

Albert Pooley

Roy Brandley

Ivan Costick

David Murphy

Micheal Piechochi

Ken Bickerton

Roy Pickard

Brian Brown

Bobby Evans

Tommy Adams

Gordon Shepherd

Peter Jobling

Vernon Jobling

Bill Stephenson

Bill Jemison

John Easton

Tony Swann

Bob Fletcher

Jamie Fraser

Terry Thompson

Freddy Thompson

George Percival

Jock Fraser

Ted Daynes

Alan Massie

John Robinson

Tony Robinson

David Taylor

Les Taylor

Ted Stokes

Peter Clemmett

Finale

Sunter's Yard

Sunter's Yard from the air.

The End
of the
Road

The final load leaving a wet and forlorn Sunter's Yard. May 1986

Reflections

In conversation with many of the former employees of Sunter Brothers, there is one over-riding impression and that is whatever else is said, the conversation always ends with a smile. Without doubt, working for Sunters was for them a series of humorous events intermingled with back breaking dirty work, long hours on the road and staying in 'dodgy digs'. Arguments- there were many, as there were the occasional fights and rough and tumbles. Men would leave the company but return, no doubt because they could earn more money with Sunters than elsewhere, but there was more to it than that. Peter Jobling actually went over to the 'enemy' Pickfords, where he admitted that the work was not as heavy, neither were they harried by the boss if not working. If times were slack they could get out the playing cards and sit around. To Peter this made no difference, there was an alien atmosphere at Pickfords compared to Sunters, and so he made his return. Ivan Costick who now 'toils' as a hospital porter says that working for Sunters was not a job, but a way of life. Bill Stephenson recalls a kindness by Peter Sunter when he was in Belgium with the company when a job had over-run and he was keen to get back home to meet relatives from Australia. Without a second thought and without any fuss or bother Peter told Bill to buy his ticket home and to make his rendezvous with his friends, with the rejoinder that he will sort out the expenses later. Bill has never forgotten that kind gesture. John Robinson who worked for fifty years with the company said that he never could figure out why he hadn't tried to do something else in his working life, but something kept him working for the Brothers right to the day he retired. Peter Clark recalls the time when he decided to leave Sunters but asked Peter the boss that he might want to make a return within a year and would he, Peter, be willing to consider him for a job then. The reply was yes and Peter Clark did return and found that his clock number had been retained until his return. Peter relates that story with pleasure. Vernon Jobling had the misfortune of having his car being taken off the road due to an accident, and when asked by Mr. Len if he was taking his wife on holiday, Vernon replied that he couldn't because of the state of his car. Len took him to a garage on the depot where there was a car that was in very good nick and offered it to Vernon, who thanked him but declined because he just did not have the money to pay for it. Len replied, "Pay me when tha' can afford to Peter lad" Vernon took up his offer and he has never forgotten that kindness.

Stories like these are legion within the annals of The Sunter Story, and will be told and retold especially when the beer is flowing. The Working Men's Club in Northallerton is now the watering hole for many of those Sunter 'reprobates'. They swap yarns of their times on the road, and even if they do not say it in so many words, they are all proud to have worked for - SUNTERS.